Landon

JUSTICE SERIES BOOK 4

KATHI S. BARTON

World Castle Publishing, LLC
Pensacola, Florida

Copyright © Kathi S. Barton 2016
Paperback ISBN: 9781629893921
eBook ISBN: 9781629893938
First Edition World Castle Publishing, LLC, May 16, 2016
http://www.worldcastlepublishing.com

Cover: Karen Fuller
Editor: Eric Johnston
Editor: Maxine Bringenberg

CHAPTER 1

Landon could see the people below him walking around the quad like nothing was going on. There was a lot going on so far as he could see, and it made him nuts to think that no one else in the world could see and hear what he could. He glanced over at the letter he'd gotten from his parents' attorney this morning and then back out the window. *Happy birthday to me*, he thought.

It occurred to him then, and not for the first time, that he should just jump. End his life. It wasn't much of one…even at nine he knew that. And now…he figured that everyone might be a little better off if he did. He knew now that his parents thought so. They seldom, if ever, had anything to do with him other than to tell him what a disappointment he was to them, and that they wished they'd given him away as soon as he took his first breath. They certainly knew how to make him feel good. Picking up the letter again, he read it aloud.

"I'm to inform you, Landon Michael Logan the Sixth, that your parents have taken steps to not allow you back into the family home. Should you try, you will be arrested on sight. If you attempt to contact my clients, you will be arrested and charged with trespassing. They have, in their words, written you out of their lives.

"Provisions have been made for your care. You will be allowed to finish your school years there at the academy, and so long as your grades are not below par, you will continue to have money in your account should you need it, but this is limited to what they feel is necessary, not you. Tuition, as well as your books, will be paid for out of that fund as well.

"At this time you have not been taken out of their will. They feel that doing so will make it so that, should they pass away too soon, you will not be cared for in a manner in which they have said. In addition, they feel it would be an embarrassment to their good name should they cut you out without anything and people were to find out about it. But there are rules that apply to you for the rest of your youth that you must abide by, or there will be nothing. You will not, however, inherit anything from their estate."

Landon knew that his name, or that of his parents, would have opened any doors for him should he want it to. But for him, it had only been a name. Nothing much to brag on, and certainly nothing prideful about it as with other families he'd seen at school since he'd been here. As long as he didn't ask for or expect any comfort or love from the two people in the world who were supposed to provide it for him, Landon had hoped that they'd forget about him. Apparently, they had not. His father was abusive, both physically as well as verbally, and his mother a tyrant, only out to get what she could from others and never give a dime back, even when it was expected of her. His parents were the perfect couple for each other as far as Landon was concerned. Picking up where he left off, he read the rest of the letter.

"At that time you turn eighteen you will be given a lump sum of cash. This money will be all that you will receive from the estate. You will not under any circumstances tell anyone of this settlement, nor will you ask for more. There simply is nothing for you. Then when you are twenty-five you will receive the rest of your money as has been willed to you by your grandfather. In the event that your parents should die at any time before the dates mentioned in this letter, this accounting will be carried out by their attorney and there will be no more funding after such time. At this time, you are their child in name only. A full accounting of the rules will come to you when it is time."

If they died? He was pretty sure that they would if any of the things around him were any indication. There were dead walking around all the time. Landon looked over at the man who was standing there staring at him. His grandfather, he'd told him the first time he'd come to him, was the only man in the world that Landon had ever trusted.

"They disown you?" Landon nodded. "Selfish shits. What do you think you're going to do as a kid? Find you a job or something? Not likely. I didn't leave them that money...I didn't leave it so they could be cold and heartless to you."

"I'm pretty sure they think they have enough reasons. You know what kind of person I've been." His grandda, a Landon too, only shook his head. Landon looked out the window again and continued. "I'm thinking of joining you. I just don't know what I have to live for anymore. I think Mother and Father would be much—"

"You'll do no such thing. Why do you want to go and do something stupid like that? You think they're going to mourn you? They will not. They'd have to have a heart to do that, don't you think?" Landon said he was tired of it all. "Yeah, I know that feeling. Got me a terrible case of the tiredness until I realized that you could see and have a nice conversation with me. What am I to do if you're not around? Now that I got you here and I'm not ready to stop talking to you as yet."

Landon watched a boy he knew running across the quad, with a bunch of the older boys chasing him. Two weeks ago that had been him. Since then he'd been hiding out in his room, only leaving when he absolutely had to.

"They're not nice here. I mean, I'm not either, I guess, but they're cruel to each other and even to themselves. I'm betting that not one person would care. I even doubt anyone here would notice me for days after I was gone. It wouldn't be me that brings them looking, but the smell of it."

"That's enough there, Landon. I don't want you feeling sorry for yourself. You should just get your ass to class and forget all that other crap. You know I got me a powerful need to see what lies that history teacher is telling you kids. If I was alive, I'd tear him a new ass, let me tell you." Landon smiled and thought that a smile shouldn't be painful like this one was. "Landon, son, don't do it."

He pulled the gun out of his pocket and held it in his hands. He heard the sharp intake of breath and wondered what his grandda would do if he were just to look him in the eye and use it. Landon had bought it several days ago, and had been surprised at how easy it had been to do so. His grandda came to stand beside him and Landon put it out to him, knowing that he couldn't touch it, wanting him to see how serious he was about ending his life.

"They don't like me. They never have. I know that I've not been the best of kids, but I only wanted them to see me. See that I'm a person too. But they never did, not when I was good nor when I was bad. I can't take this anymore, Grandda." His grandda told him that he could see him. "It's not the same. I wanted them to say they love me. That they

8

want me in their lives. But what do they do? They send me a letter from their attorney and have him tell me that I'm not to ever come home again."

The longer he stood there saying nothing, the more appeal it had to just put the gun in his mouth and pull the trigger. He knew that he could do it. He'd even read up on how his head would look when he was done. Not that it mattered really, but he did want to just end his life. Looking up at his grandda when he said his name, Landon knew that it was time.

"Goodbye, Grandda. I'm so glad that I had you in my life." Putting the small gun to his head, he closed his eyes. Pulling the trigger was as easy as opening the door, and he knew that he'd be dead long before he hit the floor. But nothing happened. Pulling the trigger again and again, he opened his eyes to see his grandda looking at him.

"Got me ways of making sure you're safe." He asked him what he meant. "Took me a person and had him come in and take the bullets out for you when I saw that you had it. Can't lose you, boy, you know that. You're all I have in this here entire world, dead or alive. I can't let you do this because of them. I had him take them out and put the gun back where you had it. Throwing them bullets away was the best thing I've done for anyone in a very long time. I can't be letting you do this to yourself, Landon. You're my grandson and I have a need for you to be around for a bit longer."

Landon threw the gun at the ghost. He, of course, didn't move, but Landon's anger spiraled out of control. As he began tearing things up, curtains from the windows, his sheets from his bed, he began screaming how his life was his own and no one else's. Then he saw the candle. Grabbing it up, he looked for matches as his grandda begged him to stop.

He wasn't sure what happened then. Landon woke up with his head spinning and the room he was in filled with smoke. The curtains were burning, as were his sheets and his books, and the letter from his parents' attorney was there as well. As he started for it, to...he had no idea, he heard the first screams and knew that the fire had spread. He'd caused the building to fill with smoke and now people were going to die. Because of him.

Landon had no idea how he'd gotten into the hallway. He was sick with the pain in his head, and his arm was hurting as well. Tumbling a few times as he tried to make his way down the smoke filled hall, he started pounding on doors to see if someone needed help out. The third door he came to was hot, but he opened it anyway. Pushing hard on the door nearly had him passing out, but he finally managed to get it open enough to see the boy lying in front of it.

Dragging the boy out by his legs wasn't easy. He was heavy for one thing, and Landon was sick now. Throwing up twice as he moved down the hall, he noticed that there was blood in his puke, and that scared him. Not that he wasn't ready to die, but that the boy with him would as well. Getting him to the stairs, he sat down, trying to get his bearings. Two boys came up the stairs toward him, their hands full of something that looked like trash bags. He pleaded with them to help him.

"Help me get him out of here." They said they had things to do. "But he'll die. I can't let him die like this. Just help me get him out of here."

"Sucks to be you, I guess." They were laughing as they made their way around him and to the next flight of stairs. Landon had no idea who they were or why they were in this part of the building, but he could see that they'd escaped being burned by the fire and soot had gotten them. Their bodies were dark with it.

"Follow me." He looked at his grandda as he stood over him, his body floating just about a foot from the stairs that he was on. "Going down with your burden is going to be easier than going up. Just make sure that you pull him by his arms and not his legs. You don't want to hurt his head any more than it already is. Come on, son, you can do this. I'll get you out."

"I hurt him." His grandda asked him how he figured that. "I set the fire. He wouldn't have been hurt if I had just jumped like I wanted to."

"You didn't do this, Landon. Not you. Them others, they did this, not you." Landon nodded and said that he had the candle and it had caused it. "No, you didn't. You might have been in the blast when it...why do you think you had a thing to do with this fire?"

"I set it. It's what I was going to do when you hit me." He told him he'd never touched him, that he'd been knocked out of the room before Landon had found the matches, that the explosion or whatever it had been had done it. "I must have found them then. I set fire to my room."

"You didn't, I tell you. You didn't do anything." Landon picked up the boy's legs and started down the stairs again, knowing that he was going to go to prison for this. And wouldn't that just make his parents thrilled. "You didn't do this, boy, I swear to you."

The next explosion rocked him. Hitting his head again, Landon knew a new kind of fear. The staircase was filled with flames now, and he was going to be burned alive, he just knew it.

~~~

Landon sat up in the bed. The dream of that fateful day as a child coming back to haunt him every night was taking its toll on him. His body was covered in sweat, and he could hear the echo of his screams in his head. Whether or not he had vocalized them, he wasn't sure. But it was bad enough that they were in his head. Again. Sitting on his bed, the shaking began and he pulled a blanket from the floor, soaked now with his sweat.

Wrapping the blanket around him to keep the chills at bay some, Landon made his way to the bathroom to warm up. He nearly fell twice on his way, and had to go to his knees once when the tremors nearly had him throwing up. His body was frozen now, his head pounding so hard that he had trouble thinking beyond getting warm. Once he was in the bathroom, he turned the water to its hottest setting, and with his back to where the mirror usually hung, he leaned against the tile wall.

"I'm here, boy." He nodded, knowing that his grandda would never leave him no matter what he'd done now or back then. "You gotta talk to somebody, Landon. You can't keep this up. You're killing yourself."

"I'm fine." Grandda snorted. It was no less than he expected of him. "You never did tell me how you like the house. Did you find your way around all right?"

"I like it right fine, and don't change the subject. Get yourself cleaned up and come on out here, and we'll have ourselves a pow-wow, you and me."

There was no point in arguing with him. His grandda had been telling him what to do since he'd been about three and no one else was talking to him. Or listening to him. When he realized that not everyone could see what he could, Landon had lashed out, hurting those that might have helped him but letting his anger at being alone most of his young life keep everyone away. He'd figured that would keep his heart safer. Not that it had.

Stepping into the hot water, he was warmed immediately. From experience he knew that he'd be doing the same thing again tomorrow, so he turned the water to a relatively cooler temperature so that in the morning his skin wouldn't be tender from his abuse today. Scrubbing his body several times, Landon leaned against the wall and thought about his life.

He was nearly twenty-nine years old, next week as a matter of fact. And it had been almost twenty years to the day since he'd blown up the building he'd been staying in, as well as two kids that he talked to daily, ones that haunted him still. And in all that time, since he'd been released from the hospital a month later, he'd not spoken a word to his mom and dad. That was until recently, when their attorney had reached out. They wanted to speak to him.

Getting out after washing his body again, he dried off, still not looking in the mirror. He would have had it removed as he had in every other place he'd been in, but he'd not figured out how to do it. Someone had adhered it to the wall, and other than busting it to get it down, he had yet to get it out of this room. Landon figured that he didn't need any more bad luck.

Looking at his body was a constant reminder of that day. The scars, old and faded, seemed as fresh and raw as they had then. No pain was there any longer, but he did feel it all the same. Steele had been the only one to see them, and he'd told him that they were barely noticeable. But Landon knew they were there. And always would be.

Going to his bedroom again, he opened the huge closet and had to grin at what was there. Or in this case, what wasn't there. The thing was as big as most bedrooms, holding not just things on hangers, but drawers for shoes and cufflinks, as well as watches and under things such as tee shirts and his boxers. Right now it had three tee-shirts hanging there, two pair of jeans that had seen better days, as well as a black suit in a bag that he'd not opened in more years than he could remember. Pulling out the worst looking of the shirts, he pulled it over his head after he'd put on his boxers and a pair of jeans. This was his attire on his day off. He headed to the kitchen, where he knew his grandda was waiting.

~~~

Logan, what most people called him, watched his only grandson move around the kitchen ignoring him. He was fine with that…for now. As Landon pulled out a big box of those flakes of corn he liked to eat, Logan suggested gently that he get him a banana to go with it.

"No thanks." They both eyed the fruit that had been in the bowl turning darker and darker since Addie had brought it to him a few days ago. "I have to go into town today. Are you going to be joining me?"

"I don't think so." Logan was sort of afraid of the town. There wasn't really anything there that would hurt him, but he didn't like all the people. It was why he'd never met any of the others that Landon worked with. Logan just did not like the living. He'd barely tolerated them when he was one of them and avoided them even now. But he didn't want the same for his grandson.

After he ate, Logan watched Landon put his things away and clean up the counter. He'd been alone too long, Logan thought. The boy was a better housekeeper than most women he knew. And when he finished drying his one bowl and spoon, Logan looked at the sad state of affairs that was his cabinets.

"You gonna get you some dishes today? Maybe a pot or two. I heard you telling that other man, Mitch, that you wanted him to come on by and have some dinner with you. What you planning to do, share the one plate you have and that bowl?" Landon said nothing, but Logan was used to that. That was another thing he didn't care for, his grandson being so lonely. "You call that attorney back?"

That got a reaction. Not the one he wanted, but enough that Logan could see that he was thinking about it. He needed to get this resolved if for no other reason than to show his mom and dad that he wasn't nearly as bad as they'd always thought. Or worse yet, as bad as they always told him he was. Landon was a good man; a great one as far as he was concerned.

"I didn't plan on it. In fact, I'd forgotten all about it." Sure he had, thought Logan, and I can pull a rabbit out of my ass. "I'll call them tomorrow."

"You'll do it now. You might have won one of them clearing house things, and they might give it away should you don't call and claim it." They both knew it was his parents, and Logan had a feeling he might know what they were gonna say. He'd been visiting them too. "Landon, call the man and get it done."

"I don't want to." He sounded five, and before Logan could point that out to him, Landon continued. "They want to see me. And then they want to sit me in a chair and point out all the things I've done since I saw them last. Twenty years is going to be a long list, don't you think? I'm not ready for that. I don't know that I ever will be."

"You're a damned grown man. What do you think you would do if they try to sit you in the corner like a child? You answer me that." Landon said he had no answer. "Didn't think so. You don't like the way they're treating you, then

15

you can leave. But you've no way of knowing shit unless you go there and talk to them. For all you know, they could be wanting to welcome you back with open arms."

"You know that's not ever going to happen." Logan knew that too. But a man could hope, couldn't he? His son and that wife of his had done them both wrong. "And what do I do, Grandda, when they ask me what I've been doing with my life? Do I tell them I start each day with you harping on me? Do I say that I work with a bunch of men just like me that talk to the dead? I'm sure that'll go over just fine."

"I don't know why not. You've made a living at it. And from where I'm sitting you've done a fine job at that too. Not the living part, but the money part. Why, you never have touched that money they paid you. Building yourself up from nothing, now look at you." Landon snorted. "You don't no more live than them ghosts you help. Hell son, when was the last time you were laid? I'm thinking it's been a long while."

"I'm not talking about my sex life with you. Especially not you. Christ." He got up and put a load of wash in the washer as he continued. "In the event you didn't notice, I just purchased this house and it's taking up a great deal of my time."

It was two more pairs of those ratty jeans he wore and five work shirts. He'd hang them on the bar when they were washed up and pull them down when he needed them. Work shirts never made it to the upper levels all that often.

"Yeah, I can see that. Laundry and dishes. Yesterday you run that vacuum cleaner until I plum thought you were going to wear a hole in the carpets. Then you dusted. If you ever want to change jobs in the future, you can make a right fine domestic." Landon said nothing, but the shirt in his hand wasn't going to survive the anger he was holding in much longer. So of course, Logan decided to push him a little harder. "You should get you one of them blow up dolls to screw. That way you can shove it in the closet when you're satisfied and not have to think about it anymore. Much like you do most of your friends."

The shirt ripped and hung limply in his hands. Logan wanted to get up and hug the boy. Hold him like he was sure no one had done in more years than was right. Logan watched his grandson struggle with his temper and his hurt.

"If I go and do this, you'll go with me? See what they really are so that I can move on with my life?" He said that he would. There was no point in telling him that this might not turn out the way he thought, because they both knew better. But Logan was forever hopeful. "All right, but you'll meet the others too. It's a fair trade for what you've been doing to me all these years."

"I can do that. But what about them boys? You gonna do something about them too?" Logan wanted to tell him to vanish them, but knew that he'd not do it. Landon had been tormented by the Bobbsey Twins, as Logan called them, since the fire.

"I don't know. You know that they come and go as they please." He did at that. Never here more than it took for them to upset Landon. Then they'd move on to some other trouble. And it mattered little to any of them that Logan knew just what had happened that day, and it had not been the way that Landon thought. And those damned boys knew it too.

The phone call from that pansy lawyer had upset Landon. Logan wanted to go through the device and choke the living shit out of the person on the other end. But he just sat there knowing that someday, not only would Landon listen to him about that day, but his son and daughter-in-law would as well. He'd been there. Logan had seen what had gone on that day and what had happened to cause it all. And it was not Landon. It had never been the boy. He also knew why he wasn't there for his only grandchild, and he was gonna enjoy seeing their reactions to that coming out too.

Landon called to set up the talk. That's what he knew it was gonna be too, a talk. He hoped that Landon would get in a few words of his own. Maybe a *fuck you* or a *fuck off* would be nice as well. Landon sat down when he closed his phone.

"I have to go there at one. They have an appointment open for me and I'm to meet him at the parents' house. I have an appointment to go to my parents' house." Logan stood up to leave with him, not that it mattered. He could pretty much go where he wanted when he wanted to. "You really don't have to go, Grandda. I was only...I was pissed off, and I didn't mean you'd have to go. There isn't any point in both of us having to suffer."

"I want to. I need to." Landon looked like he was going to say more. But Logan had a feeling he didn't want to know what it might be. "I can see how well that son of mine aged. I'm thinking not so well. What do you think?"

"I think I'd rather you just pull my nails out with a pair of plyers than to go and see them both. And if you want to know the truth, I'm sort of sick about going there." Logan knew that as well. "When this is done and you see what you need to see from them, you don't bring them up to me again. Promise."

"I promise, but on the condition that you have an open mind and don't be going in there with your head up your ass." Landon said he wasn't make any kind of promises. "Then I guess I can't either."

As they made their way out of the house and to his truck, Logan had a shiver of dread. What if, his mind kept saying, and the list was too long for him to try and work out. What if Landon's parents were as cruel as they'd always been? What if they were only bringing him there to hurt him again? The closer he got to the house, waiting on Landon, the more dread he felt. This was a mistake, he knew it. He just hoped the letter that he'd sent out would help his grandson more than he could.

CHAPTER 2

Dillon ran the dust rag over the long table again. For as much as she hated this job and how bad she sucked at it, she did take a lot of pride in it. The people that she was working for were not the nicest people she'd ever met, but they were paying her, and right now that was more important than anything. Plus, it provided her with a place to hide and rest.

The doorbell rang just as she was going to the closet in the hall. There was no way that she was going to answer it again, but she did peek around the corner when Mr. Earl, the stuffy but sweet butler, went to open it. She had a feeling that he knew who was about to enter, as the house seemed to know, but she watched and waited. Touching the little charm around her neck and holding it still, she calmed her breathing as well as her heart. Her talisman from her mom was all she had left of her. Besides, there was no point in letting the world know where she was right now.

"Mr. Landon." It took Dillon a few seconds to realize that he wasn't talking about the master of the house, but to the man with his back to her. "Shall I take your coat, sir?"

"No. I don't think I'll be here that long, do you?" Hard. Cold. His voice would have frozen icebergs, it was so frosty. "Has Dunn, my attorney, arrived as yet?"

"Yes, sir. He arrived this morning after your call. They are all in the study." The taller man didn't move and neither had Mr. Earl. "Shall I pour you a drink?"

"No, thank you. It won't do me any good to go in there with alcohol on my breath."

Dillon watched the man and wondered what was wrong. His back was still toward her, but she'd bet anything that he didn't look a bit like the man in the other room. That man was a pompous ass as well as a blow hard. His wife wasn't much better. Not that it mattered to her, but this man...he seemed to be nearly afraid to go into the other room. She looked at the woman coming down the hall and slid into the closet and pulled the door almost closed.

"Are you coming in or not? We worked this around so you could be here when it suited you, didn't we?" Again, the cold and unforgiving voice, this time directed at the man. "We've been waiting for you to show up for twenty minutes, Landon. Why are you forever late?"

"It's nice to see you too. And I'm not late, Mother, not that you'd know that about me, but I'm never late for anything. Even when I don't want to be somewhere. But it's not even one, the time I was told to show up. If you don't want to talk to me, then fucking fine. I can go back to what I was doing before you intruded into my life." The woman, Mrs. Logan, huffed but said nothing as she moved down the hall again. The man, she could see him now, only stood there with a pinched look on his face.

He was handsome. Tall with dark hair that was just a little longer than what men wore nowadays. His skin was dark, not the kind that Mrs. Logan got from the tanning bed in the basement, but like he'd spent a great deal of time in the sun with his shirt off. His eyes were piercing and dark as well. She wondered if they were black or a dark brown. When he turned and looked at her, Dillon felt her heartrate double.

She knew that he was watching her. Dillon had no idea why she knew that, but she did. But he never said anything about her snooping on him—because she knew that was what she was doing—but stood there for several seconds until he looked at the butler again, telling him he was ready. As he moved down the hall in the opposite direction from her, Dillon felt every bit of the air in her lungs move out. Holding onto the wall, she wondered what the hell that was about.

After she had herself under control again, she moved out into the hall armed with the vacuum as well as the long broom she'd use to clean the fans in the office. She hated this room in the house almost as much as she did the bedrooms that the master and mistress of the house used.

A large desk sat right in the middle of the room. Not near the window, as she might have done, or even nearer the fireplace that was as cold as the room. The large chair that sat at the desk was leather…the red darkness of it reminded her of old blood, and it creaked when she moved it to sweep. The books on the shelves were old. She had seen older, but they were never read and there wasn't a single paperback among them. For that matter, other than the paper, she'd never seen the couple that lived here read at all. And Dillon had been here for several months now.

As she made her way around the room, moving things to one side so that she could sweep the carpet, she thought about the reason she was here. Hiding. Plain and simple, she was hiding, from her father mostly. And the newspaper too.

She wasn't wanted or anything, but she did have people wanting her to find things for them. Or, as in most cases, find someone. Not a very different story than she'd heard before or even been a part of, but she didn't want to burn herself out, and found no reason that she should. The only thing that bothered her was not being with her friends, which, she thought sadly, were very few anyway.

"Kerrie?" Dillon looked up, almost forgetting that she was using her middle name to work here. She'd dropped her last name completely and switched her first to her last, so she was going by Kerrie Dillon instead of her real name, Dillon Kerrie Malone. Nodding at the woman standing there, she tried to think if she'd done something wrong again to bring the cook after her. The woman was positively horrid. Not just to her but everyone.

"I've only just begun in here." The woman, Ruth her name was, only nodded and didn't say anything else. Her face—pinched and tight—said it all. "Is there something you need?"

"That boy is here after all his time and I don't know what to do." Well, that was a first. As far as Dillon had seen the woman was always right, in her opinion, as well as never without a quick and biting remark when you thought you could speak back to her. "If he stays for dinner, then I will have to trash this entire meal that I had planned, and it was her favorite too. I'll not be having that man ruining my cooking by sitting at my table and upsetting the mistress."

And this was her problem how? Dillon wondered. Nodding at the woman, and wondering aloud what she needed her to do to help, all sorts of things ran through her mind about this place.

The man was their son, that much she knew. His name was Landon, same as the master of the house. And so far she'd figured out that neither his mother nor the cook liked him overly much, which Dillon thought might be an understatement. He was handsome and tall too. Not a lot of things that could help her in figuring out the cook's dilemma, but Dillon asked again what she needed.

"There is no help for it. Come in the kitchen and get to work is what you can do." Shocked, Dillon pulled the cord out of the wall and started to wind it in. "When you get this mess put back to rights, come to the kitchen and peel some potatoes. Then if he has to spoil my dinner, you can say you cooked it."

Dillon put the sweeper back in the hall closet and paused when she heard the voices. They were raised and angry. She could hear them all the way to where she was. She knew that one of them was Mrs. Logan and the other her husband, but when there were pauses, like they were being spoken to, she had a feeling it was the younger man. He didn't strike Dillon as one that would resort to screaming at someone to get his way. As she made her way to the kitchen, going the long away around so she could go by the parlor they were in, she saw Mr. Earl standing there with a tray in his hands. He looked to her like he wasn't sure of what he should do now as he stared to his left. And she wasn't sure, but she thought he was talking to himself.

"Do you want me to open the door for you?" He shook his head and nodded. "That's not anything I can understand for you, Mr. Earl. I can open it if you want. Ms. Ruth is going to have me peel potatoes for—"

"That is not your job." He nearly spit at her he sounded so pissed off. But he seemed to remember himself and told her again that she wasn't hired to help in the kitchen. "You are a maid, not a kitchen helper. I shall talk to her in a moment. But for now, I need for you…would like for you to go into this room with me and help me serve."

"Me?" He nearly smiled at her and nodded. "I have less knowledge of serving than I do of peeling potatoes. And I'm pretty sure you know my skills at housework. You might be better off just dumping it on them. It's what I'll do. You have to know I'm not very good at this."

"You will do fine. And we…I like you very much. Just…when they say anything, just look at me and I'll handle it. I should like for you to help me because…well, to be honest with you, Miss Dillon, I should very much like to dump this tray on the both of them, if you want to know the truth." Nodding, she smoothed out her apron and pants. "Thank you. You are doing us a great favor."

"Us?" He nodded but didn't explain. She figured he was talking about the people in the other room, but didn't ask again. Moving into the room with him right behind her, Dillon almost tripped when she saw them.

The anger coming off these people was almost as thick as the cotton shirt she had on. She could see it, almost taste it, and she could certainly see it on their faces. These people were not a happy family.

As she moved around the room, handing out a cup if they wanted it or asking if they wanted a scone, she wondered if someone should have checked for knives and guns before this meeting began. When she got to Mr. Logan, he glared at her like this was all her fault. He wasn't a man to cross, even she knew that.

"I don't know why you think this is such a big deal, Landon. Just fucking do it and shut up about it. It's not like you've done anything for us in all the time you've been alive." She heard the man, the younger one, snort and nearly fumbled her cup. It wasn't until Mr. Earl cleared his throat that she glanced at him. At his nod, she turned to look at the handsome man at the fireplace.

She'd thought him handsome before. And he still was…pretty even. But right now, with his body stiff and hard, his face blushed with his anger, she thought him the most gorgeous man she'd ever seen. At Mr. Earl's prompting, she held out a cup for Landon to take.

"No, thank you." She nodded and put the cup on the tray to move out of the room with Mr. Earl when Landon spoke again. She knew his words were not meant for her this time, but they still stung. "You've not done a damned thing for me either in all the time I've been alive. Since I got out of the hospital nearly twenty years ago, I've done just what you've demanded. You told me to keep my distance, and I have. The only reason I'm here today is because…well, I'm here because…well, if you've nothing else to say to me, then I'll be on my way."

"You'll stay here until I get what I want." Even Dillon thought that was a little ridiculous. The man had to be in his twenties, well past the point of having to do what his parents told him to do. "Sit down, Landon, or so help me I will cut you off without a penny."

The man laughed, bitterly. "You mean you don't care what your friends will think if you kick your only son out on his ass? Oh my, whatever will the social world think to find out that the Logans of Breepoint have cut their son out of their lives? Again." He laughed again. "But tell me, do you think any of them know you even have a son? I mean, it's been nearly two decades since I've even crossed over the front doorway. You think any of them remember me? I bet if I was to go and ask, none of them have ever heard you mention me. And you should know, cutting me off won't affect me in any way whatsoever."

27

"I despise you, Landon. And you'll do this or so help me, I'll hurt you in ways that those fools you work with will even abandon you when I'm finished with you." She and Mr. Earl were headed to the door when Mrs. Logan said that to her son. Dillon slowed her step and actually started to turn to the woman to ask her what the hell was wrong with her when she brushed up against the suit of armor near the fireplace.

~~~

Landon watched the woman as she started to fall. The suit was going to kill her if it fell atop her, so before he could think that he was going to catch hell for this, he nearly knocked his mother back to scoop the girl up from the fireplace and the armor. She started screaming the moment he held her up off the floor. He was sure that he'd been too late to help her.

"I got you." He tried twice more to get her to calm down, with his mother behind him telling him to take the dreadful woman away, when Landon finally had enough. Turning to his mother, Landon felt his temper snap. "Shut the fuck up, will you please?"

The room grew quiet, so quiet in fact that he could hear the ticking of the clock in the hallway. Landon looked at Mr. Earl when he said to follow him. Carrying his light burden, who was unconscious now, Landon took the girl to the kitchen, where he knew a first-aid kit used to be, as well as help should she need it.

"Is she hurt, you think? Do you think she needs medical attention, son?" Landon told his grandda that he didn't know but didn't think she'd been hurt. "I think all she did was touch that thing. Must have had something on it for her to feel all that power."

Landon sat down in the kitchen chair with the woman in his arms, and looked at his grandda with a stern whisper.

"What did you do, old man? Did you make her fall? Did you plan this?"

"No. Goodness, boy, do I strike you as an abuser of women? I'd gladly hit that mother of yours if I could, but not this little one. You tell Earl there that you want to wipe her down. She's all covered in tears." He took the wet cloth that was handed to him. "I will tell you that I knew she was here, but not much else. Poor little bit of a thing."

Ruth had never been a fan of Landon's since he'd been a little boy and had told her that her apple pie was nasty. She eyed him now with a look that one might give someone they didn't trust any more than they could throw them. He asked who the girl was, not really caring at this point what the old biddy thought of him.

"Her name is Kerrie Dillon. She's been working for us about three months now." Ruth told Earl that it had only been two. "All right then, two. That's about all we know of her other than she's not much of a maid. Very nice young woman. Polite and helps as much as she can, but not cut out for servitude."

It was on the tip of his tongue to ask why she'd been there for two months if she was terrible at her job when his father came in with the family attorney, Hayden Carney. Neither of them spoke to the other people in the room; it was as if they didn't see them. Which, Landon was pretty sure they didn't.

"Your mother has had to go out, so we'll have to reschedule this for tomorrow. I just can't deal with you any more today either. I'll expect a more pleasant talk tomorrow, and for you to have the answers I want." Landon asked Ruth for a cooler cloth and ignored his father when he spoke again. "We're going to resolve this, Landon. I don't want to hear from you how you have your own life. You're our son and that's all there is to it. It's not as if we've asked anything of you."

Landon looked at his grandda. He knew that he didn't need it, but he was asking for permission to see if this was done. At grandda's short nod, Landon looked at his father.

"I'm done." Hayden opened his mouth to speak, and Landon stood up, still holding Kerrie in his arms. "I said I'm done. I will not be moving back here to live in this house. I never liked it when I had to live here. And in the event that you don't remember it, you said I was never going to be welcome here as anything other than a guest, if that. I most certainly will not marry that woman you suggested...no, you demanded...that I marry. I won't be going to any engagement party that you've planned, and I will never, so long as I live, act like we're a loving and close family. Nothing is worth all of that. So, if you'll excuse me, or even if you won't, I'm leaving."

"You ungrateful bastard." Landon just smiled at his dad as he held the woman in his arms. He realized when looking down at her that she was awake, but didn't really feel the need to let her go. Besides, she had the most beautiful eyes he'd ever seen. His father screamed at him to look at him when he was speaking to him. "Landon, so help me, I will never speak to you again if you don't do this."

"And up until now, Father, you've had conversations with me how many times? We've not spoken in more years than I can remember, so I'm sure I won't miss it in the future. And, just so you know, I've found that I like it that way." The woman in his arms struggled, and he sat her on her feet but didn't let her go just yet. "I don't want to be contacted by you again. Not for any reason."

"I'm your father, by God." Landon said nothing, feeling better than he had in years. "This merger will help both our families. They're going to benefit with the name of Logan, and I'll get a piece of the business. And just because you don't care about money, you'll be surprised to know the rest of the world does. There is no way you can turn this down. Stop being a fool. I've offered you more than I wanted to give you."

"And you can shove that up your ass."

His father took a step from him, and Kerrie laughed. Her timing could not have been worse for her, Landon supposed. But he thought it was funny.

Just as his father drew back his hand to no doubt hit Kerrie, Landon grabbed it before he could touch her. As he stood there holding his father's hand in his fist, Landon could see the pain on his face and how much his father really hated him. And when he looked at Kerrie, as if he only just realized she was beneath him, Landon could almost feel the shift of his father's anger to her. Jerking his hand from his, his father straightened his suit and glared at her.

"You're fired." He wasn't sure if he meant her or him, but either way, neither of them were going to stick around to find out. "Get your ass out of my house, and don't expect to be paid for this either. Nor will I give you a recommendation, so don't even ask."

"Okay, that's fine by me." Kerrie looked at Landon after smiling at his father. "Can I get a ride into town, please? I don't have a car. I just need to gather up my shit and I'll be ready to go."

"Of course." Grandda laughed too, but like Kerrie, no one heard him. Landon looked at his father when Kerrie left him to get her things. "Don't contact me again. We're finished."

"You're my son, damn it, and it's high time you started to act like it. I will not tolerate your acting like you're not a

Logan. It's bad enough that I have to read about your stupidity in the paper when you go out and fleece those people. The least you could do is change your fucking name when you do that, but you will do this. Or so help me, Landon, you'll regret it." Landon glanced at his grandda and then back at his dad when he continued. "I mean it, Landon. You're going to regret this. Those men you work with, they'll be looking to your ghost for answers when I'm finished with you. Just do as you're told and no one has to get hurt."

"You're a piece of work, Father. You know that? Ever since my birthday when I turned nine, you've ignored me and didn't have a thing to do with me until today. And now when it suits you, when you finally have a purpose for my existence, you call me up and make demands. Demands that suit you and make my life hell. Again." Landon laughed. "Well, you reap what you sow, old man, and I'm over you and Mother. As I said before, do not contact me again."

As he made his way to the front of the house, Earl and Grandda right behind him, he saw that Kerrie was waiting on him. Taking her bag from her, he looked around the house, what of it that he could see, and wondered how the hell they'd accumulated so much in way of things but were still poor. Looking at his father again, Landon could almost feel sorry for him. Instead of saying anything, he moved out of the house and onto the porch that more than likely had never been enjoyed by any of the people on the inside.

"You'll be hearing from my attorney, Landon. And soon too. If you think this is over, then you're stupider than I thought you were." Kerrie looked at him now, her face full of humor, and when she winked at him, he smiled. "Are you listening to me, Landon? I'm going to get what I want. I always do."

"Good luck with that one." Landon helped Kerrie into his truck. Then he moved to the other side to get in as he spoke again to his father. "But if I were you, I'd look into a few things. Such as the fact that I don't need your money, and haven't for a good long time. Not that I wanted it in the first place. I never did. And I have the means and the ways to ruin you in a heartbeat if you fuck with me. I'm not that nine-year-old that you nearly destroyed. You might want to remember that in the future."

Landon had no idea what his father said as Landon got into his truck and started it. He thought about taking a deep breath before he moved down the drive, but decided that he didn't want to spend another minute there. And he didn't want to breathe in any more of the air surrounding them.

As soon as they were on the main street, the shaking began. Pulling over into an abandoned lot, he sat there behind the wheel for several seconds before he felt the soft touch at his hand. He looked over at Kerrie, and all he could think about was comfort. But not in the way that most had in mind. He needed her, not a hug.

She was there. Right there, and Landon pulled her to him and kissed her. Brutally. As he moved across the seat, jerking her to his lap, all he could think about was taking something, anything. When she was on his lap, her blouse torn open, she grabbed his hair and jerked his mouth from taking her breast. It wasn't painful, but he did look at her hard.

"You'll not take me this way, Landon. Not in a way that you want to hurt me because you can't hurt them." He just stared at her, hearing her words but not really understanding them. "Kiss me. Gently or not at all."

"They hurt me." She nodded and moved her mouth to his slowly. He could feel her breath, soft and sweet as it touched his lips. But he was in pain, deep heart pain. "I want to hurt them."

"I'm not them." Nodding as best he could with her hand still tangled in his hair, he licked his own lips when she did hers. "Do you want to kiss me now? Do you want me like this?"

"Yes." Her hand took his to her breast, and he moaned at the heavy feel of it in their hands. "I want to taste you."

"You can, but you have to behave. I'm not them. I want you to say that to me. I'm not them." He rocked upward, feeling her body mold closer to his. "You're very thick. Hard even. Do you want to fuck me?"

"Yes." She shook her head. He could almost taste her mouth, it was so close to his. "Let me. Please? I want to bury myself in you."

"In me or just any pussy?" He had no idea what she was asking and said that to her. "Do you want to fuck me, Landon? Or will any pussy do?"

"You. I don't know why, but no one else will do. No one will...no one will satisfy me like you will. Please, Kerrie, let me fill you." She asked him why, then licked her tongue, hot and wet, over his lips. "Again. Do it again."

"I'm not your slave. You need to remember that." He nodded, touching his lips to her when he did so. "No, you can't do it this way. If you want to taste me, then say it. You need to say it."

"I don't know what you want." He cupped her ass in his hands and brought her closer. "You want me too. I can almost smell you. I want to fuck you."

"Yes, and I'd like that very much too, but you have to say it." His mind was nearly shut down with the need to roll her to her back and strip her down. His cock hurt, heavy with the need to empty deep within her. As he rocked up again, her body swayed hard downward, and he knew that he could make her come this way. "Say it, Landon. Say it so I can come."

"You're not them and neither am I. I'm not...I'm not them. Please? May I please fuck you?"

Her yes screamed from her lips as she came over him. Landon took her breast into his mouth and bit down hard enough to have her crying out again, all the time she was riding him, her hips moving back and forth like he was deep inside of her. When she came again, screaming out his name, Landon kissed her then, tasting her climax almost like he was eating her pussy.

His. It was all he could think about, having her this way. She was his and nothing was going to take her from him. Need washed over him in waves. There were no more thoughts of his parents or their demands, nor was there anything else. Just her. And he was going to have her.

CHAPTER 3

Dillon moved back from him, grabbing at the button on his pants even as he suckled at her breast. Her need was making her crazy. Nothing in this world could have prepared her for the way she was feeling…the way he was making her feel. She didn't just want him, but found that if she didn't have him inside of her soon, she was going to die. As soon as he was free, his thick cock in her hand, she wanted to take him into her mouth.

"Help me, please." She moved to her feet as he pulled her pants down around her thighs. It was awkward and a little tight, but she watched him undress. She was wet, embarrassingly so. And when he slid his fingers into her heat, Dillon rode his fingers as he sucked at her breast again. Christ, the man was making her crazy. When she was naked from the waist down, she was pulled to his lap again.

Sliding down over him, Dillon knew he was going to hurt her. He was bigger than any other man she'd had sex with, and he wasn't gentle. She could tell he was trying, but he was a man used to getting what he wanted, and she was it right now. When he was buried deep inside of her, he held her to him as his head lay on her shoulder.

"I want to come right now." His voice was harsh, like he was struggling to speak at all. "If you move over me, take your own pleasure first, I can fuck you then, as hard as I need to. Understand? Until then, if I move at all, I'm going to end this."

Riding him was a pleasure. She started slowly at first, his hands digging into her hips, her breasts being teased by his mouth or hands, making her dizzy with the need to tell him to end them both. Wrapping her hands around his neck, she kissed him, took as much from his mouth as she wanted. And when he told her to come, his body harder than ever before under her, Dillon let go. Her body bowed back in the best climax she'd ever had as the man beneath her cried out his own.

He fucked her hard this way. His hands were going to leave deep marks on her body as he took her again and again. When he bit down on her shoulder, not hard enough to draw blood but enough to bring her again, she felt the stars behind her lids as she cried out a final time with him filling her once again.

Dillon felt herself being pulled forward. And when her head rested on his shoulder, she let out a long breath, feeling more relaxed than she ever had. Landon just held her to him, his hands making small circles at her spine, her ass cupped gently now as he rocked up into her. She was sated for now, but knew if he kept this up, she was going to come again. When he said her name, Dillon lifted her head and looked at him.

"Don't." She could see on his face that he was going to apologize to her. Or say something really stupid. "Please don't say whatever it is you think I need to hear, or whatever you think you need to hear. It was sex, nothing more."

"We didn't use any kind of protection." That had her mind go off in several kinds of directions. "And right now, all I can think about is coming inside of you again. Bare, so that I can feel every tightening of you when you come again. Not at all caring if we make a child or not. I want to feel you when you come over me."

Still looking at her, he lifted her breast up to his mouth and nibbled just on her nipple. It was erotic, her pussy soaking with it. As he suckled harder, his mouth widening over her, she held him to her as she rode him, her need spiraling out of control again. His hands were everywhere, her body humming with need to have him touch her, and he just seemed to know where. She was close. So close that she knew that coming with this man was never going to be just a climax, but a full out reckoning with sex.

When his mouth was near her, she kissed him with a kind of savage need that had her ride quicken, her climax right there on the edge. And when he slammed his finger into her tight hole at her ass, she came screaming again, her body coming apart twice before she felt him coming too.

Stars sprinkled in her vision. Her mind exploded without a single thought but to come again. And when he brought her hips to him, harder, faster than she'd been riding him, she felt her clit, swollen with need, being pinched, and looked down to see his fingers sliding along it, his thumb and finger tugging at her. Dillon didn't just come this time, but roared out a release that took her under.

When she woke, she was sitting in the passenger seat with his shirt on her…nothing else but the seat belt and his socks on her feet. Stretching a little, she realized that she was alone and that he was standing at the side of the building they were parked in front of. And he seemed to be having a conversation with himself. Knowing that he was more than likely on a wireless phone, she reached for her pants, only to find them in shreds. Smiling, Dillon wondered where he'd put her bag. The door opening had her looking at him.

Neither of them spoke, but she did look at him. He was handsome. No, that didn't even begin to cover what he was. The man was devastating. Dark hair, darker eyes. His skin was tanned, his body muscled. And even though they'd just had the most incredible sex of her life, she hadn't really gotten to see a great deal of him. But Dillon had a feeling it was just as beautiful as she could see now.

"You all right? I wasn't sure, but when I put you on the seat, I figured you didn't scream, so I must not have hurt you too much. Was I right?" She nodded at him. She was sore, but she knew that telling him that would have him looking more crossly at her. "I never meant for that to happen."

"Yes you did. Don't lie to me, Landon." He nodded and looked away until she said his name. "Are you all right?"

He looked to where he'd been standing, then back at her. She had a feeling that there was something more there than just a wall surrounding an empty building. When his cell phone rang, she stared at it, thinking that...well, she wasn't sure what to think. Other than that it was on the dash of his truck, not in his pocket. And most certainly not with him to be using it. When he picked it up, he got into the truck just as he answered it.

He looked at her as the person on the other end of the line was yelling. Dillon couldn't make out the words, but she could hear the excitement in his voice. Landon told him they'd be right there, and then put the phone back on the dash without moving. Whatever had happened, either to the other man or to Landon, he wasn't moving to wherever he was supposed to be going right away.

"My friend, his wife is in labor." Dillon nodded but said nothing. "They're all on their way to the hospital. I told them we'd go too."

"I don't know your friend. Hell, I don't know you." He looked at her legs, bare and stretched out in front of her. "Okay, we had sex, but we don't know each other."

He sat there for several minutes. Long minutes where her mind was doing all sorts of scenarios about how they were not suited, how she was in trouble. How, in the event she missed it, he was really wealthy and she wasn't even who she said she was.

"I'd like that."

She asked him what he'd like. It was the grin he gave her, the one that said that they were no longer on the same conversation, that made her wet again. "What is it you'd like, other than sex again?"

"Both. To get to know you, as well as the sex. It was...I don't think I've ever enjoyed it that much before." She flushed hotly and told him to grow up. "I could take you again. Right now, and enjoy it a great deal. I'd very much like to lay you across my bed and feast on you first. Taste your skin and creamy flesh. Sample your nipples too, feel them in my hands while I suckle just the tips. Hearing you —"

"You said your friend was expecting you." He told her he was expecting them both. "I don't know how I feel about being with a bunch more people I don't know."

"They won't hurt you or tell where you are."

She was still sitting there thinking about his words when he told her to straighten up on the seat as he started the truck. Tell. He'd said they won't tell. Before she could think to ask him what he meant by that, they were speeding down the highway and she was feeling decidedly lost. Who the fuck had told on her?

~~~

Landon wasn't sure what to tell anyone about her. He knew that she was on the run. Grandda had confessed it all to him after they'd had sex in the truck. Christ. It really had been the best sex he'd ever had, but Grandda had told him what he'd done to bring them together.

"I just like the girl. I've been to the house a few times and she's been...well, your father isn't the nicest of men. Did you know that he thinks that if you work for him, he's allowed to have sex with you, and that the women are supposed to just...? Well, that man is not my son." Landon tried to keep his temper under control while talking to Grandda, but when he went off in several directions at once, he was hard to talk to. "Your mother let him, I guess. He tells those girls that she's not putting out any more and that — "

"Grandda. I don't want to hear about my parents' sex life." Nodding, Grandda paced in front of him. "Why did you want the two of us to get together? You had to have a reason other than just to get her out of my parents' house."

"I did, I did." When he didn't say any more, Landon asked him again. "Oh. She's not human. I don't know if I told you that or not. Well, she's more than likely human, like you are, but she's got this special way about her that lets her find things. Like people, for one thing, and then there are little objects too. I thought maybe she could help you guys out or something. She's on the run. Poor thing only thinks she's out for a rest or two, and she's hiding out from the newspapers a bit. Her father, however, he's a tad worse than your own, if you know what I mean."

"You mean that she uses psychometrics." He nodded at him. "So what does that have to do with her hiding out from the papers? I hope you're not going to tell me that she's wanted for something, are you?"

"No, no, nothing like that. Just that they know about her and what she can do, and they don't let her rest up a bit. Not...she has a ghost with her sometimes. I'm not all that sure who he is. Only seen him a couple of times when I'm there, but...well, I don't think he's harmful to her, but he does watch over her a little at times. Not like I do you, but he's there when she might need him." That really wasn't very helpful in figuring out why she was hiding from her father. "Look, son. You've been alone long enough. I know that you more than likely won't marry this girl or anything, but the two of you have more in common than you realize. Not with your seeing ghosts, but with the way you were raised. She's been in boarding schools all her life. Then there is that thing with her being able to find things. I just thought the two of you could have some fun."

"Grandda, please tell me you didn't try and get my parents to marry me off to get me to the house." He looked shocked and Landon told him he was sorry. "So that part was real. They want me to merge with this other woman so they can be one big, happy, rich family."

"I'd say that's not going to happen, don't you? I've not seen one bit of happiness come out of that house since...well, before I passed on. And you weren't there that much either, so the place sort of went downhill after that." Grandda shook his head before continuing. "I don't think this girl is in trouble so much as there are people out looking for her. You know the kind. They want her to tell them things that she might not live long enough to collect on the money they're promising her. Then there is her father. He's bad news, but I'm not sure really what he wants her to find. Might be like yours. He might just want to control her."

"You mean they'd kill her, these people looking for her?" He nodded. "Why? I mean, what sort of things could she be looking to find for them that would cost her life? This father of hers, do you think he is having her hunted? That these people looking for her might be working for him?"

"Don't know. You'd have to talk to her about it. Oh, and that's not her name. It's Dillon Kerrie. I got me somebody to send a letter to Vinnie, that girl that you guys work with sometimes. Anyway, I had him sending her a little note, so that she could have some protection. I guess you took care of that. That Vinnie, she's going to be mad at me when she finds out it was me that sent it, I think. But I was scared for her, being there all by her lonesome while your dad was on the prowl."

"Grandda." He nodded and smiled. Landon had looked at the truck again and saw that Kerrie, or he supposed Dillon, was awake now. Making his way back to her then, he turned once more to Grandda. "Will you find out what you can about what Mother and Father are up to for me? I have a feeling that they're not going to give up so easily. I can see them resorting to all kinds of things. You know how Father is when he doesn't get his way."

"I can do that. I can. I'm sure that whatever it is, it's going to cost them dearly that you're not doing it. I was damned proud of you when you told them to fuck off. Nearly fell over when I saw the look on your mother's face, I did."

Now they were headed up to labor and delivery, and he reached out and took her hand. He'd given her the bag she'd had when they'd gotten here, and now she was dressed in a simple skirt that made her legs look long enough to wrap around him twice. As she curled her fingers around his, Landon felt...well, he felt pretty fantastic. Moving down to the waiting room after they got off the elevator, he paused before they were there and took her into an empty room.

"I'm Landon Michael Logan the Sixth. Yeah, a huge handle that means nothing more than a name to me. The people you're about to meet are about all the family I have. I mean, a family that I have come to love and cherish." She asked him if he thought she was going to hurt them. "No. I know that you won't. But you should know that we're all necromancers. Each of us, including the wives of my other friends. And Vinnie is a vampire. She might not be here, but I wanted you to—"

Her hand over his mouth had him licking her palm. He'd never thought of doing that before, which he supposed was a good thing, as mostly men had shut him up. But her eyes darkened and he pulled her body to his as she held onto his shoulders.

"Stop that. We'll never make it out of here if you keep this up." He told her that worse things could happen. "You have to learn to curb your desire for just a little while, all right? What do you mean, you're all necromancers? And who is Vinnie, and how do you know she's a vampire?"

"I've seen her fangs." Landon pulled her hand down to his cock, and she cupped him. "I don't really care if we just stay here for however long it takes to make love. There is a bed. And we could lock the door."

"No. And I told you to behave yourself. There are more important things going on at the moment that, believe it or not, don't have to do with sex. You have to explain yourself. In a way that I can understand." He nodded but didn't let her hand go as he rocked into it. "You are so not helping right now."

"I'm not trying to. Not in a way you're hoping for anyway." When she pulled from him, taking her hand away, he pouted. Landon didn't remember ever pouting before in his life, but she grinned at him. "Come here and let me drink from you."

"Focus, damn it. Necromancers. You said you were a necromancer. Why?" He asked her what she meant. "I mean, what do you do to make you a necro? I'm assuming you have some sort of power?"

"Yes. I can see the dead. All the time. A few of them live with me. My grandda for one." She nodded, but he could tell she wasn't believing him, or she was trying to and it wasn't working. "There is a woman in this room with us. She's only just arrived, but she's right there. I don't know what she wants from me, if anything, but she's dressed in a uniform and she has blood on her dress."

"And you can see her." He answered that he could, even though it wasn't a question. "And what do you suppose I need to know this for? I mean, it's not like we're dating or anything."

"Because my grandda said you can find people, and that you're being pursued to help some guys out." Her face paled, and before he could reach for her, she smacked him back. "I'm not going to hurt you."

"Who told you? What is it you think you might know? I'm not...who told you about me?" He told her again it was his grandda. "But he's dead. I mean, I heard about him and how he'd died some time ago. Your mother, I know her dad died about the same time, right? But your father, his dad...your grandfather...has been gone for some time. So you can't have been talking to him."

"Right, and I have. He's here too. But my other grandfather, he's moved on from what I can see. Grandda Logan has been keeping me company for...well, since I was a baby. I had no idea he wasn't alive until I was sent away when I was six. To a boarding school, so that my parents wouldn't have to see me every day. Not that they did that often, but that's where I spent most of my childhood." He took her hand in his and held it tightly when she tried to pull away. "He told me your name is Dillon Kerrie. That you spent a great deal of your childhood in boarding schools and that you're not close to your father either. And that you're a person who uses psychometrics. He thought that you could help us, the rest of the team, when it comes to our jobs, and that you and I would...he thought we'd hit it off. He was tired of me being alone."

When she backed further away from him, Landon stepped toward her. He knew that any minute now she was going to hit the closed door, and he was afraid she'd open it and leave him forever. As he matched her step for step, all he could think about was keeping her safe and close to him.

"You got this from someone. I don't mean your dead grandda, either." He said nothing, moving slowly so as not to scare her any more than she already was. "I want you to leave me alone. I want you to get away from...is that why we had sex? You think to hold me there somehow?"

"No. I don't know why the need to have sex with you made us do what we did. And it wasn't just me, Dillon. You wanted me as badly as I did you." She said nothing as her back touched the door finally. He moved quickly now, hoping to hold her there until he could explain. "You're as safe with me as you would be with anyone. I promise you this."

She was struggling with it. He could see that. And he was pretty sure that she believed him when he said he got his information from his grandda. When she looked down, tears forming in her eyes, it was all he could do not to take her away from everything and everyone and hold her tightly in his arms.

"I don't know what to do." He nodded and lifted her chin up so that he could look into her tear filled eyes. "There is only one person trying to find me, and I think it's only because I said no to him. I never...I don't think he means to kill me or anything like that, but I refuse to do anything that is going to get me into trouble. My father, much like yours, doesn't like to have people tell him no. He thinks that because he was present for my conception that he sort of owns me."

"I understand." And he did too. More than she could know. "We're going to go out there, and we'll explain to my family who you are and what you're doing with me. Then we'll work on keeping you safe from him and anyone else that comes along."

"What am I doing with you?" He just shrugged and then leaned into her mouth just enough to feel her breath on his mouth. "Don't tease me, Landon. Kiss me."

"Gladly." Taking her mouth, Landon lifted her up enough that he could feel her pussy at his cock. Rocking her against the door behind her, he rolled his tongue over hers, trying to get as much of her flavor into his mouth as he could. He wanted her, his cock, hard and hurting, wanted to be freed and buried deep within her, but she pulled his head back and looked up at him. She was pretty good at keeping him under control, and he sort of loved it.

"You're dangerous." Grinning, he kissed her again as she held onto him. But when she pulled his head back this time, he could see that she wanted him as much as he did her. "We have to do this. Not this, the sex, but go out of this room. They might wonder what we're doing here."

"I'm stone hard. I'm pretty sure one look at me and they're going to know." He rocked into her again. "Let me have you. I want to fuck you right here. Just to...just enough that I can make us both more relaxed."

"That's the dumbest pick-up line I've ever heard." He lifted her blouse up and cupped her bare breast into his hand, thumbing her nipple. "I'm going to come if you keep that up."

Turning her, he thumbed the lock on the door and made his way to the bed. He had to have her. Not when they got home, but right now. Laying her on the bed, he pushed her skirt up and then leaned down to her pussy. She was soaking wet, and he licked the first taste of her.

"I'm not going to survive you, am I?" He just grinned as he pulled his pants down to his thighs. Fisting his cock, he moved it over her clit and juices until he nearly came himself. When she grabbed the pillow from the top of the bed and put it over her face, Landon slammed forward and nearly cried out himself. She fit him. That's all he could think about as he filled her over and over; she fit him.

He wanted to take his time, fuck her slowly, and watch her face as she enjoyed it. But he was hurting and they weren't in a very private place. Moving the pillow from her face, he kissed her hard, hungrily as he fucked her, pounding her as hard as he'd wanted to in the truck earlier.

"When you come with me, we're going to have to be quiet about it." He lifted her blouse up over her breast and tugged hard on the tight nipple. "When I get you home, I'm going to take my time with you. Explore every inch of you after I eat you."

"Please. I need to come. Fuck me, Landon. Come in me." He had a thought that they weren't using protection again, but she tightened around him, strangling his cock, and he knew that she was coming. Letting his own body go, Landon could have sworn that he felt his cock releasing in her all the way to his toes. Then she bit him on the shoulder, and Landon came apart again. It was the best thing that had ever happened to him, going to his parents' house and finding her there.

Keeping his weight off her, he held her to him as he rested. Christ, he'd not had this much sex in five years, and never had he come this hard. When she opened her eyes to look at him, he knew then that he could love this woman for the rest of his life and never tire of her. As he helped her dress, then himself, Landon tried to tell himself that he was lonely and that she was nothing more than a woman he was helping, but that hurt not just his heart but his head as well. When they were both presentable, he took her into the hall again, this time holding her hand tightly in his, and she never once tried to pull away.

CHAPTER 4

Vinnie watched the two of them. Landon said he would explain to her later what was going on, but for now, she just watched her. The man with Landon, his grandda, she'd seen before, but he didn't concern her as much as the one that kept going in and out of the room, who seemed to focus all his energy on making sure that Dillon wasn't hurt.

Ghosts could, she'd only just realized, hurt you. They could even kill you if they took a mind to. Shove you into oncoming traffic. Or even whisper in your ear that you wanted to die. Some of the weaker minded people would follow through on these suggestions, but not a lot. Most of the time they would just hang out and offer up suggestions on what they wanted you to do. But this man was different. He was not even aware, Vinnie would bet, that he was watching over her.

He would keep close to her when Landon wasn't near her. Twice when she'd gone to the bathroom, the ghost had gone with her, standing outside the door until she came out, and then following her down the hall until she was next to Landon. Or one of them. Then Vinnie realized that Logan was falling in love with the woman. And the ghost knew it, Vinnie thought.

"Please don't speak to him. I don't think she can see him; or she might know he's there, but does not speak to him." Vinnie leaned back and waited for Logan to explain himself. "He's not related to her. He's someone that she was supposed to find for the family, but his body was...he wasn't happy that they were not able to find all of him. He'd been dismembered by his murderer, and the family was satisfied with what she'd been able to locate for them. But I think...do you think that he is bothering her for some reason?"

"No. I think he's keeping her safe from someone else. How much?" Vinnie asked him quietly. Logan nodded as if he knew what she meant, and she waited for him to return to her after he'd gone to see his grandson. Landon had left the room for a moment, and when Logan returned, he said that Kari was in the final stages of labor. "How much was she able to find for them?"

"All but his head. I don't think he thought they should have been happy with her not finding it. But you should know that she did try. I heard that she even went out to the site where the body had been located by herself to see if she could find it on her own. But she wasn't that lucky." She asked him if they'd caught the murderer. "Oh yes. She was able to lead them to him when they found the saw that he'd used. Left some of him behind on it, I guess. I'm not sure how all that works, you see. But she is trying to find it. You think that he's protecting her from my Landon? I assure you that he's not going to hurt her."

"I know that. But you've been watching her for more than just the few times you've seen her at your son's house." The man looked around nervously, and she did as well. The only person who might have been able to hear her was Kari, and she was a little busy right now with birthing the baby. "How long have you had your eye on her for Landon?"

"Landon is very...he's more than just lonely, but he's hurting too. Some days I despair of him getting out of the house when he had no reason to, and I think that his parents hurt him more than I thought. Not that I don't still believe that, but with her with him, he can think on other things other than...other than what he believes he's responsible for." She asked him what that might be. "You know his name and how old he is, don't you? Well, look him up. I can't...someone should have done it long before now to help him, but I don't think...no, I know that Landon would leave should someone find out. But it's all lies."

"He killed someone." Logan shook his head sadly. "Then he thinks he did. And his parents are blaming him for it."

"Look him up." Logan stood up then and moved away before turning back to her. "When you need me, just call my name. I've learned to keep myself hidden from people like you, and it has served me well. But you call me when you've figured it out and I'll come back to you."

When he faded out of the room, Vinnie sat there for several minutes, not paying much attention to the things going on around her. As she sat there, her mind drifting in and out, she started to close her eyes, and that was when she saw them.

The boys looked like preps. Both of them were about sixteen to seventeen years old when they were killed. And neither of them looked like it had been a very easy death, either. They'd been burned, and badly. The taller of the two worse than the other.

They were tormenting Landon. Not only that, but they were touching him, sticking their bodies into his until he had to get up and move. The boys, laughing now, followed him to the other side of the room and began their torment again. She had no idea what they were saying, but whatever it was, it was tearing Landon apart. His aura was dark with pain, and she wanted to see what she could do to help him. Pulling out her cell phone, she put in his name and realized her mistake immediately.

There were six Landon Logans. Clicking on each one, she read their dates of birth and death until she came to Logan. The man's picture was there with his obituary. The man had lived a very colorful and very happy life, it seemed. Not only that, Landon's grandfather had managed to nearly triple his money in a single move some years before Landon had been born, and left it all to his only child, Landon's father. And when he'd been murdered by an intruder at his home at the age of ninety-four, Vinnie had a feeling it was the saddest day in his life not to be able to go on with the next adventure. He'd been a widow for nearly forty years when he'd passed. Then she pulled up her Landon.

The sixth in a long and very prestigious lineage, Landon came from very old money. As she read about his line, his family history, Vinnie had a feeling that what might have been printed was nothing like what his real life really was. Then she came to the day of the fire.

Landon had been in Paris at an all-boys boarding school when it broke out. There were rumors that Landon himself had set it, but that was quickly dismissed when the attorneys for the family said that he'd been able to save five other boys who had been caught in the blaze that took down three of the larger dorms at the school, as well as a portion of the gym that had been the focus of the investigation. It was said, and sort of glossed over, that there had been a drug lab in the upper levels that had never been discovered until the fire happened. Two boys, both of whom had been kicked out of the school some time before, had been killed. And according to their pictures, grainy and faded in the paper, it was the two with Landon now.

It went on to say that Landon had been able to pull one body out on his own minutes after the fire trucks had arrived, and had gone in for more before anyone could guess his intent. All told, it said that he'd managed to bring out the few that had been in the building when the explosion had rocked the place, and the bodies of two who had died before help could arrive. Those two were the only deaths attributed to the fire. And Landon had been hurt badly in it as well.

She never got any further in her reading, as Steele came into the room with them. Vinnie watched his face, the way he seemed to be slightly overwhelmed by it all, until Ray snapped his finger in front of his face. And even then, he wasn't entirely focused.

"I'm a dad." Ray laughed and asked him of what. "I have a daughter. A little girl. She and her mom are...I have a little girl, and she's the most gorgeous thing. All her toes and...it's a girl. I have a little girl."

Everyone congratulated him and asked how they were doing. Steele seemed to get his act together after a little bit, and told them that she weighed eight pounds and five ounces and was nineteen inches long. That she had red hair like her mother and the bluest eyes. When asked her name, Steele turned to his sister and asked her to tell them. Aster had died at seventeen, but had never left her only brother.

"Her name is Aster Bethany Constance Bennett. And she really is very beautiful." It was a day for celebration, and everyone brought out gifts hidden around the room. Even the nurses had bought them a gift, as well as the doctor who Vinnie knew they'd helped out a couple of times. And as they made their way back to see the baby and new mom, Vinnie asked to speak to Dillon.

"Are you planning to warn me off?" Vinnie asked her if someone else had already tried that. "No. But we've only known each other today and he wants me to move in with him. I mean...we're already sleeping together, so I guess why not. So if you're planning to tell me to go away quietly or else, then I'm going to tell you to fuck off."

Her face turned bright red when she spoke, and Dillon stared at her for several seconds before Vinnie laughed. "You always say what's on your mind, or is it because of me?"

"I have no idea. I'm sort of stressed out right now." Vinnie told her she could understand that. "You're the vampire, aren't you? Married to Mitch. And Addie, she's...well, she told me she's like Steele, but I have no idea what that means. And Kari is a panther."

"That's right. And the men, all of them, are necromancers. Of varying degrees of talent." Dillon said she was a practitioner of psychometrics. "And that would be what? I kind of know what the word means, but not really."

"I can find things or people. Just with a touch. It has to be something that belonged to the person. And I don't mean like a shirt or pants, but something that they treasured. Like a ring or something close to their hearts. I know that we're portrayed as being able to find things with a hairbrush or even a button. But I can't work that way. Anyone can use a brush after you do. And a button will catch all kinds of vibes from other people with just a hug or two." Vinnie nodded and told her she knew of a couple of people like that. But sadly they were gone now. "Yes. I have done some research on my kind as well, and they don't seem to last long. Usually someone kills them, or it's too much for them and they end their lives. It's a sad...we're not very trusted, I guess you could say."

"Someone is looking for you." Dillon said that someone was, but they were harmless. "And the man who haunts you? What do you know about him?"

"I don't know what you mean. I have...who is it, do you know?" She told her what Logan had told her, leaving out the older man's name. "Crenshaw. His name was Danny Crenshaw and he's not...he's here? He was killed about five years ago over some gambling debt. But why would he be haunting me? I found him and his killer."

"He wants his head found." Dillon stared at her for several seconds before Vinnie continued. "He's watching over you. Keeping other ghosts away that might want something from you. He also pushes you into things, like safe places, I'm betting, when someone gets too close to finding you."

"He's directing me. How? And more importantly, why?" Vinnie told her that the man more than likely thought that she needed him. "I looked and looked for his head, but it's not anywhere I can find it. If they burned it, which is what the police said they'd done, then I'd still be able to go there and find the place. But there is nothing. As if his head never was lost."

"Tell Landon. I'm sure that he knows about your ghost, but not what he wants from you. Tell him and he can have some of his connections look for you." Dillon asked what she meant. "They can find out where his head is, maybe. I mean, it's worth a try. For all you know, he even knows where it is."

Vinnie waited with the young woman as she worked things out in her head. For some reason, Vinnie admired her, the way she seemed to have her shit together, even thrown under the bus as she had been. When Landon came out to get her and Dillon, she went into the room to see the new baby as well. But Vinnie had a feeling that it wasn't going to be like this forever. Things were going to hit the fan soon, and she was afraid someone was going to get hurt.

~~~

Landon showed her around his house. He had been aware of how empty it was, but never more so than he was now. There were a couple of chairs at the table he'd bought on sale a few days ago, as well as some small appliances that he'd had to have...a tea maker, as well as a tea pot to make hot tea. There wasn't much in the way of dishes in the cabinet, but he had a boxed set, a gift from Ray, as well as lots of silverware still in the wrapping that it came in. And there were lots of things left over in the kitchen that Amber, Vinnie's grandmother, had left him as well. But as for furniture, there wasn't much.

"I have a bed." He felt his face heat up again. "I mean, I have a place for us to sleep. And there are a couple of dressers in the room too. I think they match. I never really looked before." Her giggle had him smiling at her.

"You're nervous. Why is that?" He told her he had no idea. "Well, stop it. You're making me nuts with it. And this house is beautiful, filled or not. I like it. And I'm glad you have a bed. It'll make resting so much easier. Unless, of course, it's a twin. Then you're on the floor, buddy."

"It's a super king, and we'll share it. I'm a little lonely, I guess, but I don't mind being here alone." He thought of what he'd said. "I'm not wanting you to move out. I'm just saying that before you got here, it was lonely. I was lonely. I'm not going to be with.... Christ, I need to just shut up. I never babble, and here I am making a sport of it or something."

Dillon laughed and Landon felt it to his toes and back. He pulled her into his arms, just loving the way she fit under his chin, the way her hair, short and cute, felt good in his fingers. He loved everything about this woman, and thought perhaps he could love her for the rest of his days if she'd let him. Instead of embarrassing himself again, he thought of her laughter.

"You laugh so prettily. And as much as I'd like to take you upstairs to our room and break it in with you, we've been called out." He didn't want to go either. Which surprised him. He liked going out on these missions to help others most of the time.

"I heard. You're not taking Steele this time, however." Landon shook his head. "Will you guys be back soon? Or does this sort of thing take a while?"

"I'm not sure on this one. We've been called to a library that has some issues. The city thinks it's just a bunch of kids screwing around, but we've sent out some of our friends and they've reported to us that it's a haunting. We have to see what they want." She nodded at him. "You still don't believe me when I tell you there are ghosts, do you?"

"I'm not sure. I mean...I met a vampire and a panther today. I'm thinking I need to broaden my views on things." Landon lifted her chin up and kissed her gently. "You do that so well. Makes me want more and to cry at the same time."

"Don't cry." He lifted her chin back up when she lowered her head. "Don't cry. And please tell me what's wrong. Since we've left the hospital, you've been really down and quiet."

"I'm being haunted." He knew that. It had taken him a couple of hours to find out who the man was and why he was there with Dillon, but not why he was still hanging around after she'd located him. "He wants me to find his head. At least that's what Vinnie and I have figured out."

"My grandda said as much too. He is mad that no one cares that he's not whole." Dillon only nodded. "When I get back, we'll have to talk. I want to find out as much as we can about the man or men that want you to help them. I have a feeling that they're more dangerous than you think. Especially your father. He's not a nice man."

"He wanted me to find a man for him a while back. However, I found out why and I told him no and left the house. And then...there was something very wrong about the reasons he gave me for finding him. So I did a little research and found that the man is under witness protection. Or at least I think that's who they want me to find. The addresses they gave me for him were close to the ones of the man who had simply disappeared. So I asked a friend of mine, and he confirmed it for me. Even told me he was really low on the list of things people would want his information about. So I never really let it bother me. But he can be pretty insistent when he wants something." She moved away from him but didn't go far. When she looked out over the back yard, he tried to remember the last time it had been mowed, and was relieved to see that someone was on the ball for him. "How long do you think we'll be able to make this work?"

"I'd like to say for a long time, but I don't know. Will you leave before I get back? I don't want you to, if that's what you're thinking." She turned and looked at him. "I don't want you to think that the only reason I want you here is for the sex. That's really fucking fantastic, but it's more than that. I really enjoy talking to you too. And being with you. You calm me in ways I never realized I needed before."

"As you do me. And I don't want to leave here. I know that we've only been together for less than a day, but there is something really appealing about you. Not just your wonderful cock, but all of you." He laughed when she did. "I don't know how to cook and I'm not much of a housekeeper. This house is really big, and I have a feeling that it would take me several days to keep up with it. So what do you want me to do while you're gone?"

"Whatever you want. But I do have a favor. Addie knows this woman who is a great cook, but I've not had time to talk to her. I know that you have no idea how to interview for a positon any more than I do, but it would help us a great deal if neither of us had to die by eating what the other one cooked." Landon said that she could hire her too if she could boil water for tea. "I just don't want to have to clean up after myself, nor do I want to cook. I like...Izzy, Steele's cook, said she'd come over and help you with the interviews if you want her to."

"I do." He watched her, and when the doorbell sounded in the front of the house, he left her to go and get it. Landon knew it was one of the others come to get him, but saw his grandda when he got to the hall.

"I'll watch her for you. Can come and get you should something not be right if you want." Landon told him that he'd appreciate that very much. "You go on now, and kiss her goodbye after letting them others in, and I'll keep her safe for you. For us both."

After kissing Dillon goodbye several times and being teased by Hugh a good deal, they left. Landon hadn't wanted to leave his house and Dillon, but knew that with Steele and Kari both being unable to come with them, it was going to be hard enough. As soon as they arrived at the airport and got settled, Drew started to tell them what they were up against.

"Beth was out there until this morning. She had a big showing around the area where this is going down, and as much as she hated to call us in on this, she said that she wasn't going to wait for us. She's on her way back to see her new grandbaby." Everyone agreed that was the best way for her to do it. "Anyway, the library has seen its fair share of hauntings before. Not recently, but in the past. Books being put in the wrong places after they were cataloged, shelves being knocked over with no one around. But recently they opened up one of the wings that had been closed off for a couple of decades to expand the children's area, and they are getting more and more troublesome. The guy in charge of the library, his name is Barry James, he said that it's just kids that are getting in somehow and making a racket. Carlton and Donny have been out a couple of times, and they're convinced it's not kids but people like them. But pissed off ghosts. Carlton said he hadn't been able to find out why they're there either. They're not cooperating much, he told me."

As they landed and disembarked, Landon wanted to call home. He knew that he was being silly, but he wanted to hear her voice. Calling her cell phone, he wasn't surprised when he only got her voicemail, but thought he'd try her again later. Making their way to the building, all he could think about was being back home. Landon wondered how Mitch and the others did it, leaving their wives behind all the time.

"You with us?" He looked up at Mitch and realized that he had no idea what was going on. "You should see your face right now. It's all sappy and warm looking. Like a man in love."

"We only just met. Like today." Mitch asked him what that had to do with it. "I'm not sure, but I think it takes more than twenty-four hours for someone to fall in love, don't you? Besides, we have some things to work out too. Like who is looking for her and how dangerous they are."

"She's okay with what you do, then?" He told Mitch that she seemed to be. "I think that's half the battle in our line of work, don't you? Having someone that believes in what you do. And Steele said that she's a little like us. Vinnie told me a little about her and her ghost. I guess...you know about him too?"

"Yes. He's watching her...I'm glad for that. I don't think she has all that many friends. Not that I do, but you know what I mean." Landon looked around before continuing. "My parents have...they want me to marry some woman so that their companies and families can be merged."

"Did they say it like that?" Landon nodded. "Well, aren't they the nicest people in the world? I guess you didn't get along all that well. To be honest with you, I had no idea your parents were still alive. You never talk about them. Like never. Is that the reason why? Because they're so fucking nice?"

"Pretty much. We don't talk. I don't think I've said more than a dozen words to them in twenty years. If that many." Mitch nodded and stood up. "I guess we need to get this done, right? So we can get home quicker."

"You got it. But Landon, you really do look like a man in love. If you don't love her now, you will soon. She's nice too. I like her a great deal. So do Vinnie and the rest of them." Landon said nothing but stood up as well. As they made their way to where the rest of them were waiting for them, Landon thought of falling in love. For some reason that didn't frighten him as much as it had a few weeks ago. Or forever, for that matter. Being in love with someone like Dillon would be worth it, he thought. For however long it lasted, he was going to enjoy every single second of it.

The basement where the walls had been knocked down was busy with people. Not with the living, though there were plenty of those milling about. But there were perhaps a dozen ghosts—clients, Landon supposed they might be called—that looked as confused as he'd ever seen any looking. When one of them came toward him and Mitch, his first thought was that they were going to be hurt. But the man asked who they were. After telling him, twice, the man nodded to the rest of the dead.

"They don't know it yet." Landon thought that wasn't right. "I've been keeping them in line all this time, and now that you're here, I'm sure you're going to want to do things your way. Well, you can just get that notion out of your head right now. I've got this, and you aren't needed. We liked things, everything, the way it was, so you just have them set it to rights and go away."

"What do you mean, they don't know? They don't know that they're dead?" The man told him to keep his voice down, and Mitch turned to him with a look of pure shock. Landon knew just how he felt. Some of them looked as if they'd been here for some time. "Look, we're here because there is work being done and you and your friends are messing things up for them. Let them do their job and you'll get to stay; that's all there is to it."

"I don't care what they want. You see, we were here first. And as such, we'd very much like for you to leave us alone." The man actually crossed his arms over his chest as he continued. "I don't care who you think you might be, but we're happy here and we like it this way."

"You like it this way, or you all do?" The man looked confused. "You're going to have to go elsewhere to stay. This place is going to be renovated soon, and with all the problems you guys are causing, it's not going to work out for them."

"I don't care. I like it here." The ghost started forward to no doubt run though him when Landon lifted his hand. It was just a way to ward off someone, but the ghost stopped as if he'd really done it. "Let me go."

Landon looked at Mitch, who was staring at him too. The ghost was caught in his hold, like he'd wrapped him up in a chain. As he stood there struggling with it, Landon tried to think how the hell he'd just done that. Turning to Mitch, he thought for sure it was him.

"What just happened? Did you do this?" Mitch shook his head. "I'm not doing it. Do you suppose...? I have no idea what to think. Are you sure you're not holding him?"

"Nope, it's not me, Landon." Mitch grinned before he elaborated. "I think that you've met your match. As in the woman that you're in love with is your other half."

"No." Mitch laughed. "I just met her. How the hell can she be...? We're just people, we don't have mates."

"I didn't say mate, I said match. I was talking to Connie about things the other week, and she was telling me—"

"Hello? Let me go, whoever is doing this, and then I want you to leave. Then I want to know when these beings are leaving us to our privacy." Both he and Mitch looked at the man as he struggled harder against whatever bond was holding him. "Let me go right now. Then we'd like you to have them stop doing what they're doing and leave us alone. I want this wall put back up too. We can't stand having all you people moving in and out of here like you own the place. Now. Get to it."

Mitch put his fingers in his mouth and whistled. It was loud and full of energy that made Landon laugh. When everyone turned in his direction, including the ghosts, he smiled. It wasn't the kind that he reserved for friends, either.

"Now. This is what we're going to do. If you are living, or think you are, stand to my right. The rest of you to my left." It took ten minutes to get the people moving and where they thought they should have been. All of the ghosts, including the man they'd been talking to, were standing on the right hand side.

"We have to figure this out." Mitch nodded and asked him if he had any suggestions. "Yeah, we tell them. Get their names first, then look up how or when they passed, then tell them. Or show them. But that guy there, he's first."

"Randall Phillips. That's two 'l's' in both names." Landon keyed the name into the small computer he was using when the man spoke to him. "But I don't know why you think this is necessary. I'm not going anywhere. And I might be dead according to your records, but I'm very much alive and here."

Ignoring the man, he brought up the information that he needed and looked at the man. "You killed yourself." Randall shrugged. "And it says here that when the police went to your house to tell your lovely wife, you'd killed her and your youngest son. Not a nice person, are you?"

"So what? What's done is done, and I had my reasons for this. But that does not negate the fact that you are trespassing. When you leave, I expect you to have these walls returned to the way they once were as well." His name was added to the list by the police that were helping them sort things out. Landon looked around. He had a picture of the family now, and wondered if his family was here as well. But Randall stepped in front of him. "You are to leave them alone. You have no business meddling in my life."

Landon saw her then. She was talking to Hugh and looking decidedly confused. When he started toward her, Randall in tow, he knew that this wasn't going to go well for either of them. The woman had a small boy standing next to her.

"Mrs. Phillips?" She nodded and smiled at him. Landon could see the neat little bullet hole in her forehead, and when a little boy peeked out from behind her, he could see that he too had been shot. Landon had to take several deep breaths before he could speak. "Mrs. Phillips, have you been told what happened to you?"

"This nice young man was telling me that I don't belong here." Randall started screaming at her to shut up, and she backed from him. "I'm sorry. Randall hates it when I talk to other men. He gets so jealous. I tell him that there is nothing to worry about, but he has always been this way."

"Don't be sorry, ma'am. But what Hugh here is telling you is the truth. You should know that your other children, Mac and Beth, they miss you terribly as well. Not so much their father, I'm afraid." She looked at her husband, then at the little boy at her side. "He murdered you and the little one there with you. I know that you've not been told that in all this time, but you and your son have been gone for several years."

"Randall?" Randall tried to move to be near his wife enough to touch her, but she backed away from him. "What is he saying? You killed us? You said...you told me that I was hurt in an accident. And that this was limbo, and that I'd come out of it. You said that the only reason that Jacob was here with me is because I needed him, and he's not really here."

"He's lying to you to upset you. Get away from my wife." But she cut him off, probably for the first time in all their married life. Landon had a feeling that for some time now, Mrs. Phillips had an idea that he'd been lying to her all along. "Darling, don't be this way. You know that I have your best interest at heart when I do these things."

She backed from him again, this time hiding young Jacob behind her. "When did this happen? This murder?" Landon told her. "Eighteen years? I've been...my other two children, you say that they're all right? That he didn't...he didn't kill them as well?"

"They were living with your mother when this report was written. I think the paper said that they had been spending the night with her when this happened." She nodded and held the little one to her closer. "I'm sorry, Mrs. Phillips. Sorrier than I can tell you."

"He really did this to us. He murdered his own son and wife without thought to what the other children might have...." Randall started to speak, but she cut him off once again. "You aren't to speak to me again. Never. And don't you dare come near young Jacob here either. I don't know what I can do to you...how could you do this to us? How?"

"It was necessary. You weren't doing as I said to you all the time. What was I supposed to do when I'd go to work every day and you'd not have the laundry done the way I wanted it? And sometimes there was no supper on the table. I warned you about it. Over and over, I told you to keep the house up. What did you have to do all day anyway?" She didn't say anything as Randall continued. "It was either kill you, which I blame completely on you, or have to continue to live with your sloppiness. Then after you were dead, I thought I'd have to raise the children. I've no time for that either. So I took care of that as well. Had your mother not been such a bitch and called the cops on me, I would have ended all their lives for my peace of mind as well. As it was, I had to leave things unfinished, and I hate myself for that daily."

"So you planned to kill us all so that you'd live in some comfort. How lovely for you. And what did I do all day? I will tell you, Randall. I worked. I went to my job every day; even on days that you'd beaten me so hard the night before that it hurt to breathe, I went." He told her that it wasn't a job. She was only a teacher who did nothing all day. "Well, this teacher was better than you will ever be. And my salary kept us in food and clothing when you weren't working. Which was most of the time. You bastard."

When he drew back to no doubt hit her, Landon started to step in, but Mrs. Phillips put out her hand and hit him first. Some ghosts had the power to cause pain, but Landon seldom saw them use it on each other. When Randall went tumbling back, Mrs. Phillips moved to the left side of the line where others were started to fill out, and stood there with her chin held high.

It was a long afternoon. And Landon for one thought that it would go a good deal faster since Mrs. Phillips was telling everyone that would listen what her husband had done to her and her children. Because to her, he'd hurt them as much as he had her and Jacob when he'd killed her for no reason at all.

CHAPTER 5

Kari held little Aster and tried to figure out what she was doing wrong. Every time she moved her arm, even to try to get the kinks out of it, Aster would scream like it was her job. She supposed it was in a way, but Kari was hurting because she felt like a failure.

"Can I help?" Kari looked up at Dillon and wanted to crawl under the bed. "I could hear her. She sounds really pissed off."

"Steele had to go and take a phone call, and she started to fuss. I've been doing okay with her until...she hates me, I think." Dillon said that wasn't likely. "I can't make her stop crying. I've tried everything the nurses told me."

"Yeah, sometimes they like to stretch their lungs." Dillon asked to hold the baby and Kari said yes. As soon as she was in her arms, the baby started to fuss less. And more so when Dillon started talking to her like she was an adult, not in that stupid baby voice that Kari had always hated. "My goodness, what's all this fuss about? You'd think you've never been in the world before this."

Kari watched her with her daughter and tried to study each movement. When Aster quieted down, she kept talking to her in the low tones, but was saying the silliest things. Kari asked her what she was doing.

"She doesn't care what I'm saying to her, just that she hears it. Sometimes, they just need a little distracting until you can get your own bearings straight."

Kari nodded as Dillon laid the baby on the bed, still talking to her. "I changed her diaper and tried to give her that sucky thing. Which I hate, by the way." Kari sat up on the bed as Dillon checked Aster's diaper and then pulled off her gown. Kari had been stripping down too since she'd woke up, and could see that the baby had a fine mist of sweat on her as well. Why they had the room at this temperature was beyond her.

"The pacifier will come in handy soon enough, I think. But get one that's not so ugly. Pretty girls need pretty things, don't they?" As the baby was stripped down to her diaper, she started to close her eyes. When the nurse came in to check on them, she told Dillon to put the baby's clothing back on. "No. I don't think so. Her mom is hot, so she is as well. And when they're hot, like she is, then they're going to fuss until someone does something about it. You don't like it, then we can find someone who will."

As soon as the nurse left in a huff, Dillon handed the baby to Kari. As Aster settled in her arms, Dillon did the same in the chair next to her. Aster was soon asleep, her pretty little lips puckered as if she were still nursing. Kari looked at Dillon with tears in her eyes.

"I don't know what I'm doing." Dillon said that no new mother does, but you deal the best you can. "But how did you know she was just hot? I mean, screaming at me doesn't really narrow it down."

"No. But my grandmother used to tell my aunt, if you're hot or cold, then the baby is. If you've checked all the normal things and the baby still screams, then it's physical. Check for hot first, then a pin sticking them. Both, by the way, are easy to fix." Kari nodded, too overwhelmed with emotion to speak. "They're going to be back about her being almost naked. You know that, right?"

"Yes. And I'm ready for her now. Thank you." Dillon waved her off. "I'm like a basket case of emotions right now. I feel mean one second and all mushy the next. I hope you know how to deal with that like you did with my daughter."

"Hormones." Kari nodded and held Aster closer to her heart. When she was like this, it was easy to think she could be a good mom. "I have a question. Well, a few of them. It's about the house that Landon has. I have...you know what I can do, right?"

"Yes. Landon told Steele, who told me. I hope you don't mind." She said that she didn't. "So have you found something there that you think is lost? Or someone attached to it?"

"Yes." Kari had only been kidding, but she could see now that whatever she'd found, it was upsetting her too. "Landon said that there were a lot of things left by the previous owner, Vinnie's grandmother, right?"

"Yes. A great many pieces, I think. He didn't keep much on the upper floors, but most of the living room and the two parlors are what she left for him. Is it one of those pieces?" She said that she didn't think so. "Maybe you should just tell me what it is you found."

"In the kitchen there is a new—or what looks like its new—coffee maker. It's one of those kind that nearly drinks it for you." Kari nodded. And even though none of the men drank coffee, she knew that a couple of them had coffee makers in their homes for guests. "Someone used it to commit a murder."

KATHI S. BARTON

Kari didn't say anything. She wasn't even sure what to say. Not that she didn't believe her, but Kari was still sort of shocked by it. Well, that wasn't right, she was shocked all the way to her swollen feet. Steele came in then, and he was smiling until he looked at the two of them.

"What's happened? You all right?" Kari nodded. "The baby? Is she all right? I can call the doctor in if you want. I knew that I shouldn't have left the two of you right now, but it was—"

"No. It's...Dillon found something. At their house. I think...we should hear what she has to say, then call the police. I don't.... I guess we can figure that out as we go." Kari looked at Dillon and smiled. "Tell us what you know."

"Just like that. You're not going to accuse me of making it up? Not going to say that I.... I understand that you guys are different, but I just told you that someone used a coffee maker that I took to Landon's home to kill someone, and you're ready to jump in with both feet." Steele nodded and so did Kari. The woman had saved her ass as far as she was concerned. Right now she could tell them she had two heads and Kari would believe her. "All right then. I was in the kitchen making some tea. I'm not sure how you guys brew yours, but I like to use the coffee maker. It's stronger. Bracing, I guess. So while I was out, I got myself one at a second hand place. I picked it up when it didn't seem to be working. As soon as I touched it, I knew what had happened."

"Did you tell Landon yet?" Dillon told Steele she wasn't sure how to do that over the phone. "Good point. I just spoke to him and the rest of the team. They're going to be another day. Tell me what happened and I'll figure out who we can call to help us."

Kari listened to Dillon telling them what she'd seen. Then Steele pulled out his cell phone to make a call. In ten minutes, there were two officers there, as well as a retired agent that Ray had used before. The police were helpful to a point when they did things like this, but Steele had said he wanted more backup than just cops. Dillon told the story again.

"There is a middle aged man in a suit standing in the middle of the living room. He's just standing there talking. In front of him is an elderly woman and a younger man, about twenty or so. The woman is his grandmother. The man — this is from his perspective — is feeling like he's not getting anywhere with the younger one. He says that he needs to call his office. As he turns to do so, someone comes from his left and hits him with the business part of the maker…the part that holds the water, not the glass carafe. Then as he's down, the same person uses the machine on his head over and over until it's over. He dies." The officer standing next to Dillon snorted. "You can believe me or not, buddy. I don't give a rat's ass. But I know what I know."

"You really expect us to believe that you've got this magical power to just touch something and it reveals all? Wow, you should go to all the murders with us, if that's the case. We'd have them all wrapped up in no time." The agent, Teddy Drake, told the man to be quiet. "You aren't believing this, are you? What probably happened is she's killed this man, if there is one, and now she wants to blame it on someone else. I think we should arrest her for making a false statement. We don't have time for this bullshit."

When Dillon stood up, so did Steele. Kari could feel her panther run over her skin, and she laid Aster on the bed so she wouldn't hurt her if she had to take action. But all that happened was that Dillon put her hand on the officer's and he dropped to the floor. His scream was loud enough to bring the nurses and wake the baby. Kari decided right then and there that Dillon was going to be her newest best friend.

~~~

Teddy tried not to laugh every time he looked over at the officer. He'd pissed himself twice when Dillon had grabbed him, and was now nursing a bloodied nose he'd gotten from Steele when he went after his wife for laughing at him. Things for Dave Parker were not going so well right at the moment. And from what he'd just heard, they might not for some time to come. He looked at Dillon now and smiled at her.

"Did you know what you'd find when you touched him?" When Dillon shook her head, he wasn't sure she was telling him the whole truth. "I'm not going to attach your name to any of this. And since we never told him who you are, he's not going to say anything either. Not if he knows what's good for him."

"I only meant to scare him a little. What I got was...I had no idea what he'd done, but I knew that it had to be something bad the moment I touched him. He's not very...." She let out a long breath. "He's going to lose his job over this, isn't he?"

"To be sure. Even us retired guys, we know better than to steal the drugs from lock up and sell them to kids on the street. I thought for sure that you were going to tell me he'd killed this other man." She shook her head. "But you know who it is, don't you?"

"Yes. The man was there to tell them about some insurance fraud. His name is...I don't know for sure, but it sounds like Factory. I'm not always clear on all the details. The family he was talking to has the last name of something like Cotton. Again, that's as close to it as I can get without touching one of them. And the one that did the deed, his name is Mike Collins. His name I know for sure, as my dead man touched him before he died. It doesn't always work that way, but sometimes I get more than I bargained for." Teddy was writing down information, but paused when she said the last name. "You know him?"

"Michael Collins?" She nodded. "You're sure about that? His name I mean? Because he's dead. Or is supposed to be. Could that be the insurance fraud?"

"I don't know that. I do know that he is the one that killed the other man. His imprint was on the pot when I touched it. Not that it was precious to him, but he did use it for a crime." Teddy knew that she was telling him the truth, and he knew the man that had been killed as well. "I can get you more details, I guess, if I can touch the machine again. Right now it's in the garage in a plastic trash can."

He looked over at Steele, a man that he'd worked with before. Teddy had always been impressed with the young man. He was calm and poised. Even sitting there with his daughter in his arms while his wife rested was an illusion. The man was as hard and as strong as his name when he wanted to be. Teddy asked him what he thought.

"If she said that's what she knows, then I'd believe her. I can see if I can find the other man if you want. Try to find out his name." Steele grinned then, a cold calculating grin. "But I have a feeling that you already know who all the parties are, don't you?"

"Charles Markey came up missing about two months ago. His wife of nearly thirty years filed the report, saying that he'd been out working. Charlie to his friends was a repo man. Not the sort that came to your home and took your car, but the kind that would try his best to work with you to get whatever it was you were behind on resolved. We had a list of his clients that day, but his wife told us that he had planned to hit a few more that night, so he could get off earlier the next day. He's not been heard of since." Steele said that Factory and Markey were pretty close. Teddy nodded. "One of the families that he might have visited that night was Bottom."

"So you really do believe me?" Teddy looked over at Dillon and nodded. "What is this going to cost me, agent? No one just believes me without some sort of pay off. I've been down this road a few times, and no one just simply takes my word for it."

"Not all that trusting, are you?" She shook her head. "I'm going to go by the house on my way home from here. And yours too, to pick up the pot, if you don't mind. Then I'm going to go on up to the house and have a little talk to Mrs. Bottom. She's on parole and will be a little more receptive of me if I tell her we're opening some other cases. I'll have a look to see if Michael Collins is there or not. If so, he's in direct violation of his parole, as is his aunt, Bottom. Do you know where the body might be, miss?"

"Yes. It's in the well at the back of the property. He sort of told me he was there when I touched the pot. I can't talk to him like they can, but I can feel things. It's where he is, trust me."

Teddy looked at Steele when he cleared his throat. The man was smiling again, and this time it was a little friendlier.

"She's right. I had someone check, and that's just where he is. Mr. Markey is here now should you have any questions for him." Teddy asked a few and Steele got him what he needed, and then when he stood up, so did Steele.

"You're a good man, Steele. I'm sure you've heard this before, but you're nothing like your father. But then I think I always knew that." He looked over at Dillon. "I'm to understand that you're hiding out for a little while. Well, Mrs. Logan, I sure hope you get whatever it is taken care of. If you don't, then you give me a call and we'll work something out. I help those who help me, and you've done me a great service in helping me take a murderer off the streets."

He was nearly to the door when she stopped him. "You know who I am. You know that...who told you that I was hiding out? And if you tell me it was a ghost, I'm going to hit you. There can't be that many necromancers in one town."

"No, not a ghost, but then I guess I have one with me all the time. But I heard from Landon. He called me right after I talked to Ray. He said that I was to be nice to you or he'd have my liver for dinner. Never expected him to be so protective of anyone. But now that I met you, I can tell him that you were worth the threat. And as for the people trying to find you, I won't say a word. No one will." She didn't look as if she believed him, but he left her anyway with that. He'd just have to work at keeping his word to prove it to her, he supposed.

As he made his way down the hall, he thought of the people in the other room. When his time came, he hoped to Christ that there were people like the ones that worked with Ray to help him along. What they did was both scary as well as a wonderful. Teddy was in the elevator when he remembered that he was supposed to tell her to call Landon when he was done. Pulling out his cell phone, he dialed the only number he had just as the doors opened wide as he got to his floor.

He had no idea who the men were. But he did know that they were trouble. And he had a feeling it was for the woman upstairs that he'd just left. He heard the phone being answered and started talking just as the men moved in to where he was. The doors were closing when he knew that Steele had figured it out. Or he hoped he had.

"Howdy." Both men nodded but said nothing. One was tall, wearing sunglasses even in the dark elevator, and the other was rounder, not nearly as tall, with his sunglasses on his head. When round guy pushed the button for the floor that he'd just left, he chuckled out loud but felt his belly churn up. "Going up, I guess? I'm headed there too."

Neither spoke, but he looked down at his phone. Steele had hung up but had messaged him. *Are you drunk?* Seemed like a good question when he thought of what he was about to do. Teddy laughed a little at what he wrote there, but sent back a single message. *Hide her.* As he put his phone away, praying that Steele understood him, Teddy moved to the wall and slid his gun out of the holster just as both men just stood there ahead of him. He'd almost given it up when he'd gotten here, knowing that having a gun in a place like this was a bad idea. But right now, he was thrilled to death that he'd taken it with him.

As soon as the doors opened, they moved so that he could move off. He told them that he had one more floor to go up and they nodded and moved out. Just as they were out of sight, he slipped out of the door, pulling out his phone again as he went. Calling in a possible shooting at the hospital was going to get him in deep shit if it turned out to be two guys visiting their sister. But for some reason, Teddy didn't think so.

As quietly as he could, he told his friend in the Fed building what he was thinking. He was making his way down the other hallway when the first scream took his breath away. As he rounded the corner, Teddy had to blink several times before what he was seeing registered.

The two men were on the floor, their guns being kicked away from them by Steele. A big fucking panther was on top of the bigger man, and Dillon had a gun at the back of the head of the second. Teddy nodded at Steele when he asked him if they were the men.

"They were on the elevator with me. I don't know why, but I had a feeling that they were coming this way." One of the men started to lift his head and the panther snarled deep in her throat. "I guess you have this under control."

"She does. By the way, can you watch these two? I need to go and check on my daughter. Kari is a little indisposed right now." Teddy said he would and watched the two men, who had no doubt bitten off a good deal more than they could chew. Teddy moved toward the men but kept his eye on the panther. He had a feeling that it was Kari but wasn't sure.

"What's your business here?" Neither man answered, of course, but then Teddy really hadn't expected them to. Men like these prided themselves on being what they considered unbreakable. "I've had a really shitty morning so far, and you pieces of shit aren't making me all warm and fuzzy inside. So I'd answer me before I have to have that panther there tear your throats out. You can do that, can't you, honey?"

For an answer, Kari growled low and bit down harder on her man. Dillon laughed but said nothing. He had a feeling that she'd been warned by Steele to keep her mouth shut. He told the other man to answer him.

"None of your fucking business." The gun in Dillon's hands hit him hard at the back of the head. "You're fucking going to pay for that, bitch. I'm here on official business. You'll be hearing from my boss about this."

Teddy pulled out his badge. It hadn't been updated yet. It still had him marked as active. But he didn't think these yahoos would know that. As he put it in front of each man's face, he made sure to read them his badge number as well as his name. He'd pay, he was sure, but for now it was the most fun he'd had since he'd turned in his official title three weeks ago.

"In the event that you might have missed it, my badge trumps your boss all to fuck and back." Dillon reached into the back pocket of the man's pants next to him and pulled out his wallet. He caught it just as the man tried to buck Kari off. As soon as he opened it, he looked at Dillon. So they'd been here for her.

"Says here that you're an employee of Malone Enterprises. Is that right?" Again no answer, but he had the proof right in front of him. And it was scary to think the lengths that a man would go to get his daughter back to him. "Mr. Malone know what sort of work you're doing on the side?"

"Side work? You motherfucker, we're here to collect his daughter. We're just messengers for him. And I can tell you right now, he's not going to be happy about this. Not one damned bit." The man laughed, and Teddy looked at Steele when he came out of the room holding his daughter. The man under Dillon continued before either of them could say anything. But Teddy did show him what he'd found in the wallet. "It would be in your best interest to do as you're told. He does not like to have things go the wrong way for himself. His daughter is very precious to him."

Dillon said nothing, but Teddy could see her fear. He had no idea what was going on, and as far as he knew, Allister Malone only had one child and it had been a boy. Or so he'd thought until now. Testing the waters a bit, he decided to see what he could find out from the idiot. While he was talking anyway.

"I thought he had a son. Hasn't been seen in a while, but I was sure he had himself a little one of himself." The man snorted at him. Teddy kept an eye on Dillon and wondered really what the fuck was going on. "His name is Dillon Malone, right?"

"It's not a male, you nimrod, but a female. He named her that so that people wouldn't try to take his child. Pretty smart, too, except the ungrateful bitch got it in her head to run. So we're here to pick her up and take her back to her father. You work with us and I'll make it worth your while. Tell me where she is and it could go very nicely for you." Teddy looked through the rest of the wallet, finding a very old and blurred picture of Dillon. Taking it to his own pocket, he heard the man cursing. "I swear to fuck you are going to regret this. He's a very powerful man, and will not like having to come here to get his property."

"Property? Since when is a son...sorry, daughter...property?" The man just laughed. "You might want to be a little forthcoming there, buddy. You're not going to like where you're going any more than Mr. Malone is going to like you failing big time."

"I'm finished talking with you. You're a dead man anyway. And so is the rest of this bunch. See if he doesn't get what he wants despite you're interfering with his family business." The man laid his head down and closed his eyes. It was a look to make them think that he was in control and not afraid, but Teddy knew that he was terrified. The man had fucked up big time.

Before the cops came, he and Steele had cuffed both men with the help of the hospital security. Dillon had left when Kari did, and it wasn't long after that Vinnie and Beth showed up. All of them were huddled in the room when the cops arrived to take care of the men. Teddy had about three million questions popping in his head at the moment, and wanted answers to some of them right now. But Steele headed him off when the bad guys were taken away.

"She's upset." Teddy could understand that. Her daddy was Allister Malone. "She'll answer your questions, but not right now. I don't think she really believed that he'd come after her. Or that he'd send these guys to get her. She's believed all this time that he'd just let her go about her life so long as she didn't disrupt his. I guess she's just coming to realize that Daddy isn't a nice man after all."

"You knew who she was." Steele only shrugged. "I see. And when were you going to tell us? You think that having her in your house is going to get you in good with the men in blue? I don't think so. Her daddy is supposed to have killed nine cops when they didn't want to play ball in his field."

"You do have some very colorful sayings, don't you?" Teddy felt his face heat up. "It's all right. I've heard some better ones from Carlton. You should have a conversation with him and Donny."

"They're dead, I'm assuming." Steele nodded but said nothing more. "If it's all the same to you, I'll keep my conversations with the living. Being able to converse with the dead means I'm a part of their club. For now, I think I like being on this side of the deep sleep."

"All right. But you should wait until Landon gets back. He should be here tomorrow. He doesn't know who she is either. Or if he does, he's never said anything to me." Teddy started to ask him how they'd come to have her there. "They're in love. Landon and Dillon are in love."

"So he's thinking he can keep her safe? Do you know what sort of person her father is? Or what he's capable of?" Steele said he wasn't worried. He had a much larger force and more money. "I can appreciate that, I can, but he does things and never gets his hands dirty. Ever. We've been trying to catch him for decades. And I really did think his child was a boy."

"As does the world. But if you think that he's never gotten his hands into any of these deaths, then you haven't been asking the right people." Teddy looked around the room that just the two of them were in. "Yes, that's the people we need to talk to. They can get us information that you can only dream of."

"I need something that will stick before I can do what you're suggesting. Telling a court that the dead person told me that Allister killed them ain't going to get me nothing but a strait jacket and no more pension." Steele told him it would stick. "And what do you suppose he might do if he thinks that you have his daughter? I'm assuming as of right now, he's got it in his head that she's here or he'd have not sent in his goons. And let me tell you, those guys meant business."

"So do I. And he'll never know what hit him if he even tries to come between me and my family. I'm not one to fuck with even on a good day, Teddy. Trust me on that." Hard words. Believable words too. Teddy, a seasoned officer and agent, felt his own balls tighten to his body. Steele Bennett was not a man that he'd fuck with. "Landon will take care of this. And when he does, you're going to have the same respect for him that you have for me. I swear to you, no one in my family will be harmed by this. And I count you in that circle."

Teddy left then. He had paperwork to fill out and questions to answer. For now, at the suggestion of Steele,

Kerrie Logan was the only name that would be on the report for who was present. The rest...all of the other information that he had and didn't have and more than likely never would, would have to be held back. Like the fact that Allister Malone was stretching his arms out to a little town in Ohio.

CHAPTER 6

Landon sat very still. He wasn't really sure he could have moved much anyway. He knew that his knees were a little wobbly, as well as his hands. And sitting on them hadn't done a thing to calm them. Landon looked at his grandda when he said his name.

"You all right, boy?" He said that he was, but that was a lie and they both knew it. "I'm telling you the truth, Landon. Just like I did all those years ago. You did nothing wrong, other than to be in the wrong place at the wrong time. Them idiots that were there on the stairs, they caused the fire themselves, and when they passed you on the landing, they were headed up to see about their drugs. The second blast, the one that took their lives, that's what caused the fire to spread like it did."

"They killed themselves, and all this time they've been haunting me as if I had done it to them. They played me. And you said that Mother and Father knew this? They knew all along that I didn't have a thing to do with the fire." Grandda nodded, his face full of sorrow. "How did they figure it out, or how did they find out? Not from me. I assumed...believed them when they told me it was my fault."

"The police and fire marshal then, they found the lab on the upper levels. Those boys had been doing some pretty big business from there, and most of the campus knew it. Didn't say anything because they figured it wasn't hurting them at the time. Then when you were in the hospital, that policeman that was there with you when you were in surgery, he told your parents about the lab and the point of origin for the fire. They knew then, even before you were out of recovery, that you were as innocent as they come. They just...I'm guessing that they needed something to hold over you, and that worked out just fine for them." Landon picked up Dillon, who was sitting next to him, and held her on his lap. He'd never been a hugger before, but needed her touch more than he did his next heartbeat. He explained to her what his grandfather was saying. "I've been trying to tell you this for so long, you have no idea what a relief it is to have you finally listening to me."

Landon wasn't sure why he was now, other than he had been asked by Steele to listen to his grandda, that things needed to be cleared up before they could deal with all the other stuff, such as Dillon's father coming for her. He had no idea how this tied in with what had happened at the hospital today, but his feelings for his parents had gone downhill with every word his grandda had told him. Not that he'd had a great deal of respect for them before, but now, right at this moment, Landon thought for sure that he hated them both. He looked up at his grandda when he started pacing. It was sort of nauseating watching him pace. It was hard, and without regard to what he was walking through.

"There's more, isn't there?" His grandda paused and nodded, and Landon closed his eyes. When Dillon wrapped her arms around his neck, he told her he didn't think he could take much more of this. "They have been holding it over my head since I was nine years old that I was a murderer. They even told me how they'd worked hard to keep my name out of the paper so that I could have a life. That I owed them. The other day, when I went to see them, Father actually told me that he would bring it all up again if I didn't do as he said and...and marry this other woman."

"You don't owe them shit; you know that, right? They aren't worth the lint in your pocket for all that they've done to you." He laughed and held her tighter to him. "Landon, do you know why they did this? Why they thought to control you? They couldn't have been planning this marriage. There has to be something...something a great deal more than just holding this over your head for shits and giggles."

"Yes. They hated the fact that I refused to do what they wanted. It's because I could see Grandda. I mean, from the very start, I could see him. It wasn't until I was sent away to boarding school the first time that I realized that I was different than the other kids. I had...you should have heard my mother when I told her what I could do. She had me examined by several doctors and then put in the hospital for an extended rest. What sort of rest did she suppose would 'cure' me? I have no idea." Landon looked at Connie and Aster when they joined his grandda in the room. "I have the greatest friends, did you know that? I wish you could meet them."

"Tell me about them later. Right now you need to know everything so you can move on with this. This is going to end with these people, even if I have to hire Kari to eat them alive. I'm sure she'd do it. She's scary when she's a panther. And then you and I have to talk." He knew that too. Steele had called him on the way home to give him a heads up on what had happened with Dillon and who her father was. "Landon? Are you sure you want me to stay here? I mean, my father, he's a lot meaner and carries out what he wants with force and a bullet."

"Yes. I love you." He had never in all his life said that to anyone before. When Dillon shook her head at him, he nodded. "I do. I honestly do. And as soon as we're alone, I'm going to show you how much I love your body as well."

Connie cleared her throat and smiled at him. She had become such a dear friend to him, and someone that he'd come to enjoy talking to more and more of late. He wished he'd known her when she was alive, and thought of her like someone would a grandmother. A best friend that you could go to and would never judge you. Just as his grandda was to him.

"Allister Malone is coming here. He's not happy with what happened to his men either. We've been watching him, keeping tabs on him when we figured out who Dillon was." Landon wanted to tell Connie that he wasn't sure he could take any more bad news, but only nodded and held Dillon. "He knows that she's here. There was a picture of her that hit the papers the other day. Not on purpose, but it happened when someone had shot a picture of Old Things, Vinnie's antique store, and Dillon just happened to be coming out when it was taken."

He told Dillon and felt her stiffen in his arms. "He's not going to get you. He won't come close to you either. He's a fucking moron if he tries to. Steele and I have taken all kinds of precautions to keep everyone safe. And with the network of ghosts we have helping us, he'll never get close enough to even breathe the same air you do before we can take care of him."

"I don't think you understand what sort of person he is. I mean, do you have any idea who he is? What sort of things he's done that he's never been arrested for?" Dillon got up, and Landon looked at Aster when she said his name.

"I have two people looking into his life. And a few more keeping tabs on his movements. He won't be able to go anywhere without one of us knowing about it, like you told her. But you should know that the people that he's killed or had killed, they're not going to rest until he's on their side." Landon told Dillon, and she said nothing to him. "Let her go, Landon. She needs to work this out her way. She's stressed out. We all are. We have seen what he does to people who cross him. You have to find out what he has in mind for her. And why she has until now believed that he'd not hurt her." He had an idea what the man would want with someone like Dillon...the things, the information that she could get for him with a simple touch. She was a gold mine and a liability at the same time.

"Dillon, why does he want you bad enough to send those men after you?" She paused in her pacing but never answered him. "Aster, Steele's sister, said that in order for us to help you, we'd have to know it all. Why does your father want you home? And will go to such lengths to get you there."

"I know where the bodies are." He thought that she was kidding, but when she turned and looked at him, he could see that she was serious. And afraid. "All of them. I was in his office one day when I found his gun, the only one that he's ever used since he began his career as a criminal. I only picked it up to see...I don't know, I wanted to see what the big deal was to carry one. I had no idea until that moment what he'd been doing. No, no, that's not quite true...I think I might have known, but didn't want to believe it. He caught me standing there with it in my hand."

"And since he knew what you could do, he assumed correctly that you'd found him out." Dillon nodded but didn't come any closer to him. "How long have you been running from him?"

"Not long, not really. About four years. It's been easy to keep ahead of him. At least it had been. I would stay somewhere and work and move on when I got the urge to get going. It paid off well. And I'd been at your parents' home for about two months when I got the feeling again. Just before you arrived and we met, I was ready to run again."

Aster told him that she'd been moving ahead of her father because of the ghosts. They knew that she was afraid and had been whispering in her ear when he got too close again. They'd been protecting her because she'd been helping them with the things she could do. Landon nodded but didn't tell Dillon just yet. He felt, and rightly so, that she'd had enough for one day.

"That day you fell against the armor; what did you feel? I'm assuming that was why you were screaming." She nodded but looked away from him. "It's something to do with my parents, isn't it? They did something with that thing and you know it. I want to know. Please, I have to know."

"Two people were killed using the sword that is attached to it. Their bodies are burnt to ash nearby. But their hearts are...they keep them in the body of the armor. In the feet of it. I could feel their pain, hear their screams like I was witnessing their deaths. I don't know who they are, but I'm sure you can figure that out after I'm gone." He asked her where she thought she was going. "I can't stay here, surely you can see that. If he comes here, and I've no doubt that he will, you'll all be hurt or killed and it will be my fault."

"No one is running again." Landon stood up and made his way to her as he continued. "There will be no more running from our problems. We're going to face them head on and together. I'm not going to let my parents get away with shit anymore, and your father is going to have to deal with some rules from now on. We're fucking adults, and we're going to make a stand."

When he was in front of her, she smiled up at him before speaking. "You sound like you should be speaking softly and carrying a big stick." He kissed her nose. "My father, he's not a nice person when people don't do what he wants. I know firsthand that he's the type to come in guns out and ready before he wants to see your side of the situation. Not that there is any other side but his own, but I think you understand."

"I do, and fuck him." She laughed. "I'm serious. Fuck him and my parents. I'll contact someone tomorrow about the ghosts there, and we'll get my parents taken care of before he gets his ass here."

"And in the meantime, what do we do to get ready for his arrival?" Landon picked Dillon up and headed for the stairs. "This isn't what I meant, Landon. Don't you have ghosts here that need you?"

"No. They can go away too." He did turn to look, and could see Aster giving him a thumbs up and Connie laughing. "They're telling me to go for it. And to have a good time. I plan on it. Several times, as a matter of fact."

As soon as he entered the bedroom, he knew that she'd made some changes for them. But for now, he had other things on his mind other than the decorating skills of his future wife.

~~~

Dillon bounced twice on the bed when he tossed her onto it. Before she could scramble away from him, he had her ankle in his hand and was pulling her toward him. Her pussy soaked just that quickly, and she moaned when he put her foot on his hard cock.

"I want you to touch me like this when my cock is bare." She moved her foot while he took off his belt and opened the fly on his pants. As he pulled his pants down to his thighs, she moved her foot over him again and curled her toes around him. "Christ, do you have any idea how much I want to be buried inside of you?"

"I'd rather have you eat me. You keep telling me that you're going to, but you get sidetracked too easily. I'm feeling a little left out." Dillon screamed when he pushed her foot away and tore her pants off. She was naked from the waist down when her body was jerked to the side of the bed and he dropped to his knees. Sitting up on the bed enough to see him, she knew the real meaning of the word smoldering. He looked like a starved man, as well as one that was determined to get all that he could. Dillon felt her body heat just from his look. "Landon, you're going to make me come if you keep looking at me like this."

"Good. I want you to come so much that I get my fill of you. Then I'm going to take you, hard and fast, before I make love to you over and over again." He leaned down and licked her inner thigh, and then nipped at her skin. When he sat up, she was nearly breathless when he lifted her legs up to his shoulders and then leaned slowly down to her pussy, watching her the entire journey. "Come for me, Dillon. Let me drink deeply of you."

As soon as his tongue touched her clit, she came. It wasn't fulfilling, just the opposite. It had her needing more, craving so much more than he'd given her. But when he suckled her clit into his mouth and his finger entered her, Dillon came again, her body so tense she felt every nerve ending when she came. Screaming out her release simply because she couldn't have stopped it if she tried, Dillon opened her blouse and cupped her bare breasts.

He didn't just eat her, but he feasted on her. She came so many times, every second it seemed like that she was beginning to think he'd never get his fill of her. Every time she thought she couldn't take any more, he'd bring her over the edge of sanity again and again until she was sure he was trying to kill her. Then he stood up over her. Dillon knew then that she was well and truly in love with him.

As she'd already ripped the buttons off her blouse and her bra was up over her breasts so her hands could be busy tugging and squeezing her nipples, Dillon lay bare before him. His cock, thick and hard in his hand, was leaking at the tip, and every time it touched her skin, she felt as if she were being branded by it. She wanted to take him into her mouth, even sat up to do so, but he told her that he wanted to come inside of her. To make love to her like this. But that's not what she wanted or needed right now. She wanted all of him.

"Come on me, Landon. Let me feel your hot cum all over my body. Then you can fuck me. Take me again and again." His hand moved up and down his shaft, the precum on the tip no longer a stream, but now he used it as a lubricant to come on her. "Come on me while I bring myself."

Dillon slid her fingers into her pussy and nearly came just watching him give himself pleasure. She was so swollen, her clit so sensitive, that she knew that she wasn't going to last. As soon as Landon reached up to hold onto the canopy above him, she felt the first spray of his release. It was hot, scorchingly so, and she screamed out again when she came with him.

"Come," he commanded her as his cock and balls emptied. "Come again with me. Come now, Dillon."

She did, coming up off the bed with her fingers pinching her clit so hard that she knew it was going to be sore. As she screamed, not holding back at all, she felt his hands move hers, his mouth sucking her clit as she screamed again. It was too much, her vison blurred, and she blacked out for a second. And when she felt his cock enter her, not realizing that he'd moved again as it slammed deep inside of her, Dillon wrapped her body around his, her feet at his thighs, her arms at his back, and hung on. She knew it was going to be the ride of her life.

He fucked her hard, each stoke of his cock like being hammered by him. She felt him touching her throat, her heart, and her mind each time he pulled away to fill her again. When he came, begging her to come with him, she did, her body simply letting go, and he took her away. The last thing she thought of as the lights went out was that she loved him. With all her heart. And that she could never leave him.

When she woke she was alone in the bed. There was enough light from the moon shining in the room that she could see that she was alone in the room as well. Moving to get something to pull on, she picked up his shirt and slipped it on. Not bothering with anything else, she made her way out of the room and down the stairs. She heard him speaking before she nearly entered the room.

"Grandda and I know the real story now. And the fact that you've lied to me all these years."

Dillon paused outside his office, not sure if he would appreciate her walking in on a private conversation. But before she could leave him, he spoke again. "I'm sure you thought you were just having a good time, but you took advantage of me and its stopping now. I have a wife now, and I'm not going to be worried from now on as to whether or not you harm her. Or try to."

The boys. Dillon had heard about them. The kids who had been tormenting him his entire life. Vinnie had told her a few days ago, and also mentioned that Landon had never mentioned them so she hadn't. When she heard her name, it took her a few seconds to realize that he was calling her in and not just talking about her.

The shirt she knew was long enough to cover her bare butt, but not much else. Also, since it was dark there was no way for anyone to see that she was also braless. As she entered the room, Landon was sitting behind the biggest desk she'd ever seen, and there was no one else in the room. Smiling at him, she sat down as demurely as she could in the chair across from him.

"My grandda and I are talking to Jake and Jason. Brothers from when I was younger." Dillon nodded, watching him as he stared at something, or someone, to her left. When he turned back to her, he was smiling brightly. "Grandda wants to know if you're happy here. He seems to think that you want more out of the house. I'm not sure what he means by that, do you?"

"I think I do. You could use a real table and chairs and some new towels, but that's about all. Unless you like having lawn chairs in the dining room, that is." She smiled at him. "Why does your grandda think I don't care for the house the way it is?" Landon looked to her left again, and she knew he was listening to his grandda. It kind of freaked her out just a little, knowing that he was talking to someone that was not really here. "May I ask you something? It's about Jake and Jason."

"Sure." Landon grinned at her. "Grandda said he heard you cursing the other day about the fact that the house could use a better hot water heater, as well as some warmer towels would be nice. He thinks that you're going to bring my house and me up to code."

"He's not supposed to be snooping around listening to me....wait, was he in the bathroom with me?" Landon laughed and said no, he'd been in the bedroom looking for him. "Oh. I'd like a rule if you don't mind. No ghosts in the bedroom while I'm around, please. I don't know how long I'll be here, but for now, that'll suit me just fine."

"You're not leaving me." Before she could comment, Landon continued. "We were just talking to the boys, as they've been called since I was younger, and telling them it was time to move on. I've been...well, I've been visited by them enough. Don't you think?"

"I'd say so. And I think you should deal with your parents too. Same as I'm going to do with my father." She started to apologize when Landon laughed. "I'm not trying to say what you should do with them, but I think they need to repay you in kind for how they treated you all these years. Revenge is a sweet thing, sometimes."

"I agree. And so does Granddda." Dillon looked in the direction that Landon was, wishing that she could see the elderly man as well. "He wants to know if you can do him a favor. He wants you to go back to his house that my parents live in and get something for him. He said that Earl will allow you in because you've never been banned from the house, just fired."

"I don't understand the difference. I'm assuming this is some sort of rule to keep the others from getting into trouble?" Landon nodded. "Okay. So what does he want me to get? I won't steal for him. I mean, he is a ghost and all, but I'm not. And I'm pretty sure that if I told the police who told me to take something, they'll have me locked up faster than I can say boo." Landon told her it wasn't stealing if it belonged to him in the first place. "Oh. Okay then. And Mr. Earl, he's a good guy. I don't think he'd turn me in."

"No, he wouldn't. And so you know, he and Grandda planned for us to meet. Not the way we did, but that we should meet. They were matchmaking. And I, for one, am glad that the meddling old fart did it." Dillon told him she was as well. "Good. Anyway, my parents are set to go on a short vacation in the morning, and Mr. Earl and the rest of the staff will be giving the house a nice fall cleaning. He knows to meet you there and he has a package for you. I don't know what it is, but Grandda assures me that it's not too heavy, and that you should be able to carry it easily."

"And the other issue, the one with the boys, is that resolved?" He looked around the room, then back at her, shaking his head. "I see. So they plan to haunt you for the rest of your days then. There should be rules about this. Something that will get them into trouble."

"There are. I plan on telling Steele that I want them banished." That sounded...well, that sounded really final. As she looked around the room again, she wondered if Landon could see them as they were or how they had died. "Dillon, ask me whatever you want. I might not have the answer for you, but I will try to help you understand."

"Why can you do this? I don't mean what you do, because you have to. I understand that more than anyone. But why can you do this? Were you hurt at some point in your life? Did you, I don't know, did you die and this is the result of it?" She looked around again in the dark room. "I could always find things with a touch. I can't find a person by touching another person every time, but sometimes. It's sort of hit and miss, mostly miss that way for me for some reason. Why you? And why can you?"

"Let me...I need to explain something first. Okay, the rest of the group is a good beginning. Kari can do it because at one point she had died. It was from an infection that had set into her skin, and she was already weak to begin with. Something about Steele not giving her what she needed during sex. I'm not entirely sure what that meant, and I sort of stayed out of it when she was better. Vinnie could because she was born a vampire and she's mated to Mitch. Again, I'm not sure how the two are intertwined, but that works for them. Addie was already a medium. She could do things with her mind that others couldn't. Sort of what you can do, only a little more. She's as strong as Steele is."

"And how do you rate the strength of what you are? Hard core, like Steele? Somewhere between okay and poor? I'm not really...I don't know what I'm trying to ask you really, other than, can you do some things that even Steele can't?" She waited for him to answer, knowing that it was a hard question. "I know that there are others like me out there. Some are stronger—not many, but a few—and then there are the ones that have no talent at all that claim to have it. Those people give me and the others a hard time of it. I'm sure you have the same thing. But I'm trying to gauge what sort of power it is you have."

"I was born this way. As were the rest of us men. And yes, there are varying degrees of what we can do. Like I said, Steele is the strongest I've ever seen, and he seems to get stronger daily, especially since he's married to Kari. I'm not sure, and neither are the rest of us, if it's because of what she is or that he's so relaxed now that his true self is coming to fruit. His mother is too, but not as strong as him. Addie is still learning what she can do, but she's very close to what Beth and Steele can do. And as you know, there are different things that each of us can do that the others cannot." She asked him what his talent was. "It's kinda strange really, and not all that helpful most of the time."

"Show me." Nodding, he stood up and moved to the wall that was filled with books. As he lifted his hand up, she moved to stand beside him just as several books came down from the uppermost level and floated to her. "You can levitate."

"Sort of. What I can do is control a ghost that might be close and use his energy. I don't do it often, as it's draining on them." She asked him if he'd used his grandda. "No, the boys. I try to wear them out like this so they don't come around very often."

"Brilliant plan. I'd be lifting cars if that kept them from me." She put her hand over his heart when he pulled her into his arms. "We really need to sit down and talk. I'm not asking for a commitment from you, because frankly being with you scares me a little when I think of how fast this is going."

"Me too. Mitch said that you were my match. I asked Billy about it. He's Beth's father, and he said that there is one match soulmate for each of us, he believes. Not everyone is lucky enough to find them. He said he had, but there are few really that do. They fall in love, marry, and have a long life, but that doesn't mean that you were a match. He thinks we are as well." Dillon looked up at him when he lifted her chin. "Dillon, I know that we haven't known each other all that long, but I think you are my match. And that I love you with all of my heart."

"I've fallen in love with you as well. But I'm afraid. It's too perfect, and in my experience, perfect is not always a good thing." He held her then, and she could hear the beating of his heart and knew a comfort that she'd never had before. "Landon, can we please go and buy some towels today?"

Laughing, he told her that was on his list. "And I have a man coming in today to see about a new and bigger hot water heater. I talked to Alexandra, the woman I bought this house from, and she said that she'd never used it much so hadn't thought of it."

Dillon didn't ask. She wanted to, but she knew there was going to be a long story about how he had gotten a house from a woman who didn't shower much, and right now she wanted to bask in his love of her. Landon was a wonderfully loving man, and she was going to keep him for as long as he would let her.

CHAPTER 7

Allister didn't have a clue why his daughter would choose to live in squander like this when he had a perfectly good cell just waiting for her to fill. Having her run free like she was scared him, and not just a little either. She knew entirely too much, and that was going to get her killed. Or him if he didn't get her where she needed to be. As he entered the house that he'd purchased a decade ago and had forgotten about until he needed to come here, he thought about his other business here. Might as well get it over with while he was here, he thought.

Glancing at Mable, he starting clicking off the things that he wanted to get done. Allister had been trying for years to trip her up, give her too much too fast so that she'd miss something. But so far, and it had been years and years since they'd been together, he'd not once been able to do it. As she wrote, seemingly not missing a thing around her either, he paused at the door to his floor before exiting the elevator.

"She's here, right here. And soon I'll have her just where I want her." Mable said nothing, but he knew that she wasn't thrilled about being a part of this, or the other business he was going to take care of while he was here. "And make sure that the Logans know that I'm in town as well, so that they can begin the process of kissing my ass. This plan that is in motion needs to be taken care of as well."

"Mr. Logan called here this morning, and I assured him that you were going to see him. He is most displeased with things on his end." He asked her what it was now. "I'm not sure, sir. Something to do with his son. I don't think Mr. Logan has a very high opinion of his son, and would like to discuss the issues with you."

"I don't have time to hold his hand every single time he has an issue. Didn't I just get him out of a mess recently?" Mabel said that he had. "Well, tell him that I want to see him, but if he brings up anything about that kid other than he's doing what he's told, so help me I'm going to kill them both. Why is it that our children just don't listen to us anymore? When did they get to the point where they think they know more than we do?"

"I'm sure I don't know, sir. Perhaps with all the things going on in their lives that they are better at it than us. My son and his computers are—" He cut her off. Allister didn't care about her personal life as long as it never touched his. "Yes sir. I'll get on that right away."

As she walked away to do what he'd told her, Allister entered his room. It wasn't the nicest home he owned, but it would do. All he really needed was a bed and access to some Internet and he was fine. But he'd worked his way up from the bottom, and he wasn't going to scrimp now on the things that he felt he deserved. And Allister had discovered that he really did like the finer things in life.

His computer was set up on the small table near the window, and his clothing, he knew, would be pressed and hanging in the closet just as he liked it. His toiletries were all lined up in a neat row, and his bottles of shampoo and other items he used once and tossed out were where he could reach out and touch them should he want to. Everything Allister wanted was just the way he demanded it every time. It had better be if they wanted to continue working for him.

Sitting at the small table, he pulled up what he wanted to check on. Yes, the plane was ready to leave when he was ready, and the flight plan on standby in the event that things got hot here and he had to leave. Allister tried to be ready for anything to come his way, and if he wasn't, then there were ways for him to get them.

His appointments were lined up, dinner reservations were confirmed, as well as the times that his suits were to be picked up and returned for cleaning should he need it. There was an appointment set up to speak with not just the Logans, a meeting he was not looking forward to, as well as a meeting to see the chief of police. A man that he needed to make understand that he was going to be very disappointed if there was any backlash from him taking his daughter out of town when the time came. Also, he had to deal with this other person, Bennett, whoever the hell he thought he might be in the big ocean that Allister controlled. And he did, every single ounce of it.

His men, sadly both of them, had met with an untimely death. Mackley had been killed in a tragic boating accident that was still under investigation. Allister wasn't worried. He had good men in place for this sort of thing, and knew that no one would know that he'd been dead long before the boat blew up. And Pinkerton had a massive stroke, one that was brought on by eating too much lead. Again Allister wasn't worried, but he did mark those things down as doing business with an unknown. And he planned to get to know Bennett very well before this was finished.

Allister had money stashed all over the world. Not just in the houses that he owned, but also in banks under assumed names, with identification as well as passports to go with them. Hotels that he owned and had maintained under so many layers of red tape and bullshit that he knew that no one would ever find it. And if they did happen to stumble over it, he'd have been there and long gone by then.

Not just money either, but large caches of jewels and drugs. Things he could readily sell should he not be able to get to his money. There was a plane at every point of the world, always ready and always updated with the latest of everything, including women should he need them.

Boats graced the finest harbors, houses that he owned were well maintained, kept up yet never lived in. He could simply get on any mode of transportation and be somewhere that was safe, money at his command, and a whole new identity. Allister Malone was ready for anything. Anything, that was, until his daughter came along.

He remembered her standing in his office like it was yesterday. She'd been about eighteen or nineteen then. Allister had only just stepped out of his office to take care of the body he'd had to deal with. The man, he couldn't for the life of him remember his name or why he'd pissed Allister off so badly. But his daughter no doubt knew, and that was what had him searching for her night and day.

"What are you doing, darling?" He and Dillon had been close, closer than most daughters and fathers. She was his world; they did everything...well, most everything together. "Where did you get that, honey? Guns are not to be trifled with, you know that."

He'd tried his best to blow it off. Make her think that he'd only just found it in his desk. He knew, after minutes of her just staring at him, that something had gone terribly wrong while he'd been away from his desk. Allister asked her if someone had called and had said something to her.

"You killed them. All of them." He laughed. His body hurt with the pain of her finding him out. "Daddy, how could you? That man was only trying to make a living, and you killed him?"

"Who have you been talking to, Dillon? I want a name right now." She backed away from him when he took two steps to her. He'd always known that she could do what she did. As long as it had never affected him directly, he didn't care. But that day, her touching his gun, it had changed everything. For them both. "Dillon, I want you to put that down right now. Do you hear me? You've no reason to be.... Are you afraid?"

"Yes. Of you." That shocked him, right to his very core. "You're not a very nice person, are you? You never have been. And you lied to me."

His temper was something he prided himself of having complete control over. Even then he'd been able to maintain his cool, and thought that dealing with her in a straightforward sort of way would be the end of it. He'd bring her up to speed, and she'd be able to help him in ways that he'd never imagined she'd be doing for him. Little did he know then that things were about to get very hot for him. And all because of his daughter.

"So? It's about time you figured it out anyway. I'm going to need for you to take over some of the projects I have soon enough when I'm away or can't be bothered with them. Darling, you and I are going to make so much money you'll have everything you ever wanted." She put the gun behind her and backed away from him until she was near the outside doors. "Dillon, what did you think was going on here? Where did you figure all this money was coming from?

The tooth faerie? Christ, child, it's been hard enough just trying to keep you out of it, but now that you know, well, things are going to change. And for the better I think. Come to my desk and I'll...you should really think about your next movements, child. I'm not a happy man when I don't get my way. You should have figured that out when you picked up something that didn't belong to you."

"I'm leaving here now. And I don't want you to ever contact me again." He nodded, thinking that she'd just go to her room and forget about it in a couple of days. "I mean it. I'm not going to live here with you ever again."

He looked at her then, wondering not for the first time if he should have smothered her at birth. She was his baby, his pride and joy, but he'd known since her mother left them...when she'd been killed...that Dillon was going to be a problem someday. Even Mabel had commented on the fact that little Dillon was brilliant and might be something of an issue for him when she got older. Dillon had looked at him in a way that her mother had in that moment before she'd been killed. "You are a murderer. You killed that man and all those others because of drugs or money. I don't want you to come near me again."

It had taken Allister hitting Dillon in her face with his fist to get her to calm down. He'd not liked doing it to her. But she was screaming about calling the police and other branches of the Feds, and he'd been terrified. So in order to calm her down, he'd hit her, then locked her in her room. It was three days before he realized that not only was Dillon gone, but so was some of his money and his gun. She'd taken the evidence with her when she ran. That was when Allister's love for her had turned to hatred, and he had to find her to shut her up.

The phone ringing startled him out of his musings. Picking it up, he said nothing until the person on the other end spoke first. When there was a soft chuckle at the other end, Allister started to hang up. Prank calls were not high on his list of things he wanted to deal with today.

"I wouldn't if I were you. Hang up, I mean. I'm not one that you want to piss off any more than you have." His heart rate doubled at the sound of the man's voice. "I assure you, it will not go any better for you if you hang up on me now. Especially when we've gone to so much trouble to talk to you."

"Who is this? How did you get this number?" The man laughed again. "I demand that you tell me who you are. And what you want."

"So many unanswered questions. And they will remain so until I get what I want. Why are you here, Allister Malone? You thinking that you can bring your daughter to heel?" Allister nearly dropped the phone. The man sounded like he didn't just know what he was doing here, but what he had planned once he had his daughter. "You should know that she's not going to come to you. I could say not easily, but the truth of the matter is she's not going to go anywhere with you."

"I'm not going to ask you again who this is. Tell me, damn it." He was beginning to hate the laughter at the other end of the line. And the man behind it. "Fuck you. You don't know shit."

"Don't I? You are currently sitting in your big office with a nice view of the pool in your back yard and a garden that is gorgeous. But I doubt very much if you'd notice. Not that there's all that much else to look at with the fence all the way around you, but there you have it. You have on a blue suit, which I must say is kind of out of style, as well as a dark green tie. You had wanted the gray one, but there was an unexplained stain on it and you had it burned. Tisk tisk, there Allister, what a waste of money." Allister swallowed hard and looked around for the cameras. "There are none. Cameras, I mean. I'm having you watched, but not with cameras. You should know that you've been on my list long before you left your home at nine-twenty seven this morning, seven minutes later than you wanted, and the man that you hit because you needed someone to blame is being questioned about a great many things going on in your household. Also your driver, who is in custody at the moment and talking like it's his business to take you down. Which, you might like to know, he's only touching the surface of things that I know about you."

"What do you want? I have money." The man said he did too. More than he did. "I can give you whatever you want. Anything."

"Anything? That's a tall order, don't you think? And I doubt very much you'd give me what I want anyway. But I will take a great deal from you." Allister told him he would. "All right then, I want you to go to the police station and turn yourself in. For everything. Like the murder of the lawyer that showed up to your house to have you stop using the neighbors pool for your own little late night fuck parties. Or the couple that you had working for you who had the nerve, in your opinion, to ask for a day off when his mother passed away. I believe you told them that time was money and you didn't have time to spare it on stupid excuses. Their death hurt a great many people, including their grandson, who misses his grandmother dearly."

Allister gripped the cell phone tighter in his hand. The man knew entirely too much, and there was only one person in the world that knew that much. His daughter. Dillon had ratted him out to who knew who, and now they were coming for him. Standing up, he nearly wet himself when the man told him to sit down.

"Now. I'm assuming that you have no intentions of giving me anything." Allister said he wasn't going to jail. "No, you're not. You have too many people who want you alive for you to be stuck in a jail cell where they can't get to you. Well, some of them can't. There are a few that can get to you even as we speak. And they're waiting for the day when they can tear you apart."

Allister tried to control his temper. He prided himself on his ability to control all aspects of his life, and here he was on the verge of not just losing it, but also his mind. This man knew things that not even his daughter might know. Like the stain on his tie. The fact that he'd killed his housekeeper and butler when they threatened to go to the state about him refusing them time off. And there was the fact that the man seemed to know just what he was doing every minute of his conversation with him.

"I'm going to hang up now, and when I do, I'm going to have this call traced." The man laughed again. "You won't think it's so fucking funny when I come to your house and kill you and your entire family, now will you? Then I'm going to find my daughter and shoot her between the eyes for making it perfectly clear that she's not only not to be trusted, but no longer a daughter to me. I will end her before I ever step foot in a prison, if I ever will."

"Let me save you some trouble. My name is Steele Bennett, and I live three miles due east of the house that you're staying in. Which, I would like to point out, is a major stepdown from the one you consider your main home. Would you like my phone number?" As it was being rattled off to him, Allister tried to think where he'd heard that name before. "And so you know, if you come here with any kind of malice, you will regret it for the rest of your very short life."

The line went dead. The sound, the long hum of it, had him as shaken as the man's final words to him. Carefully and slowly, he put the handset back in the cradle and sat down. Allister was as scared now as he'd ever been in all his long life.

~~~

Steele laid his cell phone down and waited. Billy was supposed to come right to him when the phone was hung up and leave Carlton behind in the hotel room to watch Allister. The two of them had been watching over the man since he'd figured out who he was to Dillon. Almost as if he'd summoned him, Billy appeared in the room with him.

"He's powerfully pissed off." Steele told him good. "Threw up several times, almost not making it to the commode too. Funniest thing I done ever did witness, and you know that I've seen a great deal. You suppose he might come here after all?"

"I hope so." Steele looked over at the tiny cradle that his little girl was sleeping in that had been brought in here earlier this morning. Kari and Dillon were out shopping for things for the house. Vinnie had some people watching over them, as did he, but he knew that if anything came their way, Kari could tear the man apart. If it came to that. "Grandda, do you know if his wife is around? On my side or yours?"

"She died some time back. Right after she birthed up that girl of Landon's. Broken heart I heard, but don't know. I've got my feelers out for her, but you know that if they don't want me to find them, then I can't. Connie is looking too, just to be sure." Steele had a feeling that she'd been broken rather than just broken hearted. Two of the nurses that had attended the birth of Dillon had said that Allister had been thoroughly pissed when Dillon had been born a girl and not a boy. And more so when he'd found out that there were never going to be any more children. "Steele, what do you think of that girl, Dillon? Heard tell she can find anything she puts her mind to."

"I'm thinking of asking her to dinner tonight, her and Landon. They've been avoiding us all since she came to his house, and I'd like to get to know her. Kari loves her, and her somewhat jaded view of children. She told Kari that she'd had a nanny that had a baby, and that was how she'd learned about children. I guess her father never paid any attention to her or the nanny, and it was several years before anyone knew that there was a baby in the house." Grandda said that he loved her ideas on child rearing. It was spot on with what his own wife had done with theirs. "Kari said that Dillon has a wealth of information about a great many things. She's well read, she told Kari. I think it's more than that."

"I'll look into it for you. Maybe I can find me some answers from that guy that you have in that safe house. That driver of Allister's, he seemed pretty talkative to that guy you have watching him." Steele told him to look into it for him. "You should also know that Landon is having a conversation with his tormentors. Not sure what he's going to do with them, but that's what I heard."

"He told me that he's going to have me banish them. There is justifiable cause. They've done nothing to help others, and they've been a nuisance since the day they were killed. I told him I'd do it. He has only to say the word." His grandda told him that was a good idea. "Thanks for helping me."

"Anytime, you know that. I'm always up for some fun." Grandda laughed. "I'm thinking I need to go and have me some fun with Connie for a bit. That woman can surely make me laugh."

After Grandda left, Steele sat there for several minutes. He was thinking of the boys that Landon had always had with him but never mentioned. Whatever they had been to him, Steele figured they were his problem. At the time, Steele had had enough of his own issues he was dealing with. Now he realized he should have stepped in, at least asked him about them.

Steele thought of the other issue he was having taken care of. Vinnie's father was still around. Not much of him was left; the man had not taken care of himself since he'd been killed, and now he was nothing much more than a wad of chewed up gum that would stick to your shoe. Steele was going to go out later and deal with him as well. It was time for him to move on, to wherever that might be.

"Are you babysitting all by yourself today?" Steele looked up at his sister and smiled. To have her back in his life, even like this, was the next best thing to having her there in person. "I just saw Kari and Dillon. They're safe and having a good time. I think Vinnie and Addie are going to meet up with them later."

"Landon was telling me last night that they're out of even the smallest of things. He hired a cook today on the recommendation of Izzy. Did you know that she has a sister?" Aster said that she did as she peered into the cradle that was softly moving back and forth. "Oh, I have something for you. Something I think you'll love."

"Do you?" She didn't turn around to see him, so when he came up behind her, she turned and stepped back. "Steele, what are you doing? You hate it when we get this close."

"Not you I don't. But take me." She frowned at him. "Take my body and pick up your niece. You know you want to hold her. And I want you to."

"No, that's not...you said that it's dangerous to do that with her. It would confuse her." Steele touched his fingers out to his sister's cheek and wished, as he had so many times, that he could hold her once more. "Back up and let me around you. I don't want to go through you, but I will."

"Take me, Aster, and hold your namesake. She is awake and will be crying soon, and you won't want to hold her then." Her head was shaking, but he could tell she really wanted it. "Either take me or I do you. And you know that you won't have as much control if I do. Hold your baby niece. Tell her that you love her and hold her in your arms."

She moved into him. It was soft and inviting, and Steele felt his own eyes fill with tears. Her happiness hit him first, then her sadness. Not at holding his child, but that she had to come to him for this moment. Her love for all of them was so much. Steele could feel his sister's love for him and Kari, as well as the baby. He knew that she was saddened by how much she was missing, and how much more she would as well. But she could see them, she told herself, which was more than most other ghosts could do.

Steele hoped that Aster could feel his love for her as well. How much he missed her, needed her in his life even still. His heart was still heavy when he thought of the things he'd said to her the day she'd been killed, and he knew that for as long as he lived, he would cherish her as much as he did that day. As she reached into the crib to pick the baby up, he knew the moment she touched the baby that his daughter knew there was a difference in the two of them. And her smile was enough to make Steele feel like he could take on the world and come up a winner.

"Oh Steele, she's so pretty. Look at those eyes. Just like Mom's." He could speak to Aster this way, but was so overwhelmed with emotion right now that all he could do was feel. Little Aster was staring up into the face that she knew, but she seemed to know that it was someone special holding her. Steele figured that his daughter was a great deal like he and his sister were. Maybe even more.

"Kari said that she's got a lot of her panther in her. Not a full blood of course, but a great deal." Aster said that she'd talked to Kari too, as well as the baby. "You need to come to her more often. I think she can see you."

"Of course she can. And grandmother too. Grandad has taken to telling her stories at night when she wakes up." Steele knew this. He'd heard him telling her the most farfetched stories over the baby monitor that he'd had set up in her room. He also knew that Kari was sleeping better now too, knowing that the baby was being watched over by so many people who loved her. "She's like us, did you know that?"

"I thought she might be. I know that as a child she can see and talk to any of you guys, but she seems to be able to summon anyone she wants as well. Like Grandda when she wants him close at hand, as well as Garth. He loves coming here to see her."

Garth was a young boy that had been murdered by the same people who had tried to kill Mitch when he'd been a kid. Garth, a ghost that had been around for a while, had known what the Bruces were up to, and had stepped in and saved him and another boy. Garth had been buried in the back yard with several other young boys, without so much as a marker to say he'd been killed. Steele had had him brought here when his body had been exhumed, and his marker had been placed just last week. He had been helping

Mitch with some of the projects he had going. It had worked out well for all of them except the Bruces, who were set to go on trial for murder and all sorts of other things in three months.

When Aster said that she was ready, he knew that as soon as she left his body, he was going to feel slightly drained. And as Little Aster was put in her crib, his sister moved out of his body and stood nearby as he held onto the closest chair. When he was stronger, he turned and looked at her.

"Thank you so much." He nodded and wiped at the tears streaming down his face. He thought perhaps that his love for her had doubled in the last few minutes. "No one could ask for a better brother. And you're going to be such a wonderful dad to her. I'm going to make sure you are, by the way."

"I expect no less of you." She nodded and looked around before standing close enough that he could have touched her if he could. "Aster, I'm so sorry every day of my life for saying those things to you. If I could have taken them back, you know that I would."

"I know that. And I know that you didn't mean anything. You were stressed. We both were. And I promise you, Steele, I never once thought of it again after I left the house. I was free for the morning and doing what I loved. Being me." He nodded, still brokenhearted for her. "I love you so much, big brother."

"And I love you just as much, little sister." They stood there for several seconds, each of them, he was sure, lost in their own thoughts. When she lifted her head to look up at him, he could see her happiness as if she were really standing in front of him. "Come to see us more, all right? I need you around more."

"I will. But for now, I have to go." He nodded and watched her fade just a little. "Tell Dillon that she's going to be just fine with us. I think she worries that Landon is going to put her to the curb soon."

"He loves her." Aster nodded and faded a little more. "I love you. Very much."

"And I you." Then she was gone. Steele went to the crib where his daughter was sleeping, scooped her up into his arms, and sat in the newly purchased rocker and cried hard as he held her to his heart.

CHAPTER 8

"So how does this work?" Dillon watched the couple in the other room who were telling another officer what had happened to their only child. It was all lies, she'd been told, and they just needed her to prove it. The man behind her, however, was less than helpful, and getting on her nerves. "You just go in there and tell them that you've located their child and that you want them to come clean with his murder? I don't see that working. And the courts will throw it out in a hot minute. Tell me again why the chief thinks you can do a better job than we have so far?"

"It would help me if you would just let me think." Really, she was terrified of being here. Landon had asked her to help out the police with this case, and she wasn't sure how she could help. But Teddy, she'd been told, had asked for her. She could do no less than go in there and do her best. If the man complaining all the time would just shut the fuck up. "Just be quiet and let me think."

He snickered a little and leaned back against the wall behind him, as if he were humoring her. She supposed he was in a way. But she knew things that he didn't. Like the little boy that they claimed was kidnapped was actually dead. By their hand. The reason she'd been brought in,

Landon told her, was that they couldn't locate the body. But he thought she could.

Landon and the rest of the team had been called out late yesterday afternoon. She and the other women of the family, including, she'd been told, Connie and Aster, had ended up at the mall at the kitchen store. She'd not realized that there were so many things you might need in a house as big as the one that she lived in with Landon, but the new cook, Alice, had given her a list of things to get. And she told her that if she wanted to have a hot meal in the house, that things were going to need to be brought up to this century. The stove alone was nearly a hundred years old. Then the call came in from Landon.

"We have a problem that I think you can help us with." She said she'd try. Then after he explained what had happened, she told him she wasn't sure about that. "I am. You can find people, right? With the right things that belonged to them?"

"Yes. I can find anything that has some sort of attachment to the person. But it has to be theirs, not something that the family has picked up at the store because they think that'll work." He asked her what she meant. "A few years ago this family lost their child. And they didn't have his favorite toy with them. I think it was with the child when they...never mind. They thought if they got the same toy and loved on it all the way to the offices, then I'd be able to just use that. Sometimes people think it'll throw me off, too. See if I'm lying about what I can do."

"Well, that's...I guess I can understand people not believing what you can do. But the other? How the hell did they think that would even work if the kid had never touched it?" She told him she had no idea. "People are just plain weird. Me included. But Teddy thinks there's more here than they're saying. Even the cops are sort of stumped on this. Can you help him out?"

So now here she was, in a large police station with hundreds of people milling around the place while she tried her best to get her courage up. She was afraid to find the child, and more than that, she was almost sick with knowing that the people she was going to have to go and talk to had done it to him.

"I'm ready." The officer stood up but still acted like this was all a game. Going into the room with the people, she introduced herself as Kerrie and nothing more. "I've been asked by the police to come in and see if I could help out. I'm a medium. Do you know what that is?"

The man looked at his wife and smiled. It was a smile she'd seen before. It said, "Yeah, right, she's here to help them." Not that it mattered what he thought of her. Right now she was doing the right thing when he had not.

"You want us to tell you what happened again, and then you're gonna touch us and see that we're telling you the truth. All right then. So long as it brings us back our little boy, we can play all the parlor games they need before they really start to look for him."

She told him that it didn't work that way. "I need to touch something that belonged to him. Not to the family, but to him. Like a blankie if he has one. Or a favorite toy. Even a bottle will do."

He asked her if a diaper would do. "I got a nice ripe one in the car that might help you." He stood up then, his body hard with anger. "You think you can just come in here and make demands on us when our child is out there suffering at the hands of some kidnapper? We don't even have his blankie to keep us comforted, and you're asking for a diaper."

"I never asked you for a diaper. I told you something that belonged to him. You're the moron that thought a shitty diaper would help in this in any way. Now shut up and get me what I asked for." The man stared at her and the woman cried. The woman, Teddy had told her on the way over here, was the stumbling block for whatever had happened. She had no idea what that meant, but hoped she was wrong about the child's demise.

Dillon made it a point not to know the names of the people she was working with. Or for. She wanted to have a clear picture of whoever she was looking for and what they might have been to the people looking. Same with items she'd been asked to find. Just that a watch was missing, or a wallet. Nothing more, just the basics. Now she wanted to hit the man in front of her. But the mother pulled out a worn stuffed bunny from her pocket.

"It's his. It's J—" Dillon told her no names. "He slept with it. It helped him to sleep. I found it in the car when he was...when those people took him from us."

Nodding, Dillon asked her to put it on the table. As she was taking deep breaths, the man said he wanted her out of there. When he reached for the little toy, the cop stopped him.

Picking it up in her hands, she knew several things about the dolly. First of all, this particular toy had belonged to two other children before the missing little boy. A little girl had loved it, as had a child with a handicap. She wasn't sure what his handicap was until she concentrated harder on him.

It was their son. As she held the bunny tighter, she closed her mind to the conversation that was going on around her. The woman was crying softly, but the man was getting louder by the minute. When she heard him cursing, Dillon started speaking. She figured that if he knew what she had found, he'd shut the fuck up.

"Your daughter was born with a birth defect. It wasn't caught until she was nearly ten years old. But that didn't stop you from locking her in the shed at the back of your property and letting her starve to death. Her breathing was making it hard for your husband to hear his programs, so that had to be taken care of. This bunny was all you had left of her." If the people spoke, Dillon was no longer listening to them. It was the person that had loved the bunny that was. "The second child that you put in the shed was younger. He too was born with a birth defect, but not as bad as his sister's. You actually thought about keeping him around for more welfare money because it was hardly noticeable, but in the end, the father hated that Mommy had given birth to a retard. Then the third baby came along. Trevor was born with congenital heart disease, just as the others had been. You killed him a little differently in that you put him in the bottom of the well when he was only three months old. The only reason that you're claiming that this child was taken is that you had him in a hospital, where the other two had been birthed at home. The men, as you call the welfare agents, were going to wonder where he was when his next doctor's appointment came up and he wasn't around." The pain in her head brought her out of the memories. Then blackness took her under.

When she opened her eyes, she was lying on the floor and her body was covered by someone's jacket. She'd been hit, she knew that much, but why or how was a mystery. When Landon picked her up, holding her so that she could no longer see the table, Dillon asked him if she'd helped.

"We didn't know about the other children until now." She nodded. "How did you know that much? I mean, the children...how did they know what was wrong with them?"

"They didn't. The mother did, and she's been holding onto the bunny longer than the children had. Her memories were on it...little of the children, as a matter of fact." Landon nodded and held her to him. "What happens now, Landon? Will the parents be brought to justice?"

"The mother confessed while you were out. The father, he tried to shut her up but ended up being cuffed and taken away before she finished. She told them everything, including where the other two bodies were buried. She'd done it for them, wrapped them up and buried them while her husband slept."

"What else?" He frowned at her. "There is a reason that you're keeping me like this. What is it?"

"She's dead." Dillon asked him who. "The mother. When the police were trying to talk to her, one of them got too close, I guess. She pulled a gun free of one of their holsters and shot herself in the head."

"Have you been talking to her?" He told her that Steele was, as he was stronger. "Tell her that the children loved her. All they thought about was...they knew their father hated them, the little girl especially. But they loved her. Very much."

"I'm not sure that she needs to hear that right now. I think she's telling him that she had been living with the guilt of this for some time. Since...well, the oldest. I don't understand some people. Why not just give them up for adoption?" She told him what she knew as he told her that he'd only just arrived when she'd been hurt. "So they didn't let the welfare office know that she was dead. And the other child, how did they account for him?"

"They didn't. He was never born, so far as anyone knew." Landon led her out of the small room and out into the sunshine. She paused there, turning her face to feel the heat of it on her face. "Landon, I love you. Very much."

"I love you very much too. Will you marry me?" Dillon turned to him. "I had this really awesome speech all made up in my head. Things I was going to say to you. Share with you. But seeing you here, with your face bright with the last rays of the day and the shadows of the night coming on us, all I can think about is having you as my wife and growing old with you."

"Yes. Yes, I'll marry you. But I have one favor to ask of you." He nodded and came toward her. "I want to adopt children, as well as have them. I want to give some child or children chances that they seldom get in this world."

"I love that idea. And yes, we can do that. I have everything arranged at the courthouse for us to be wed in the morning. I don't want to wait around until something goes wrong again." She laughed at him. "A man has to do what he can when his future wife is right here and willing."

~~~

Allister wasn't having any luck. Or fun. There seemed to be a trip-up at every turn. And no one, not a single person around him, knew his daughter. Yet he knew she was here. Strolling down the street thinking about how poorly he was sleeping, he stopped when he saw the shop in the newspaper article. Old Things.

Personally, Allister hated old things. Antiques were not his thing, and he avoided things that even looked like they might have been from another era. Distress made him think poorly, and he wanted no part of that. But he had to admit, whoever was in charge of their display window had a knack for it. It was appealing, yet much understated. He thought he'd see about hiring them for one of his store fronts.

"Excuse me." The woman behind him was pushing a pram. He'd bet his last nickel that she'd gotten it in this place, because it looked as old as the building it had more than likely come from. Opening the door for her was a mistake...he was pushed inside just in front of her and ended up standing in the biggest warehouse of old shit he'd ever seen in his life.

"Mr. Malone." He put out his hand before he could think that the man standing next to him shouldn't know his name. As the man took it in a hard, unforgiving grip, Allister thought of the man he'd spoken to yesterday. "Welcome. I see you're getting around all right."

"Who are you?" He hated the way his voice screeched. The way his palm felt sweaty and hot when the man finally let him go. And worst of all, he hated not being on top of things. He liked to be the one with all the answers.

"Landon. We were told you might be around today. I do hope you go back to your main home soon. We've no use for you here." Allister felt his temper rise, and he actually put his hand to his side where he knew he had a gun. But the man laughed at him. "That's no longer there. I don't want it to go off and hurt someone that might be in your way. Your gun will be returned to you when you get back to your plane. If you plan to see things my way, that is."

"You stole my gun?" The man only laughed at him, and Allister felt the hair on his arms dance. "Give that back to me right now."

"I'm afraid that would be breaking the rules, don't you think? Not to mention felons aren't supposed to own guns. That ten years you spent in prison should have taught you at least that much." Allister took a step back, then another, until he bumped into someone behind him. "Allister, I'd like for you to meet my good friend, Steele Bennett. But then, I think you've spoken to each other."

Allister turned and looked at the man. If anyone had been named for their appearance, this man was it. He was hard looking, ruthlessly so. The word "unforgiving" came to mind, as did a few others. If he were to be doing business with this man, Allister knew that he'd not live long if he crossed him.

"I've come to bring my daughter home." Landon and Steele both laughed. "She's mine, and I'll do and say what is best for her."

"She's my wife." Allister felt his balls tighten to his body so tightly he was having difficulty swallowing. He'd never realized that the two things were even closely related. His cock, if he had to piss, would be difficult to find. He knew that it had crawled up into his body so high that he'd have to wait until he was relaxed to see it. "And as for you owning her or whatever it is you think you have over her, I don't think she sees it that way. Dillon is pretty strong-minded when that sort of stuff is brought to her."

"You can't have married her. I would have heard about it." The man, Landon, didn't comment, but only cocked a brow at him. "You think you just get away with this? How dare you. I'm in charge of what—"

"How dare I what, Allister? Marry the woman that I love? It's been done before, let me tell you. Do it without you knowing? Well, that was a bonus for us both. We kept it quiet because we wanted to. Now, as for your plans for her now that you know where she is, if I were you, I'd think about your next move and leave while I could. You never know what might happen to you should you fall in with the wrong people." Allister asked him what he was talking about. "Landon Logan...he's my father."

"No." Landon nodded and smiled. Allister had all sorts of things he'd like to say to this man, but all he could think about was that his daughter was with a family that had caused him nothing but issues for decades. But he could not believe that for all the planning that he and the Logan's had done, his daughter was married to a Logan anyway. "You married her to blackmail me. Well I won't have it. I did exactly what your father wanted and got the two of you together, and he is going to pay up, or so help me I will ruin you all."

"You think so? I don't. You'd have to get by me to get to Dillon. Not that I don't think she could take care of herself, but if you do tangle with her, you might be surprised to know that she's not the kid you ran off when you murdered those people. Oh, and you might want to consider that she still has the murder weapon. What do you suppose she should do with that?" Allister knew she had it still. He'd just be too lucky for her to just have left it somewhere. "Ah, here is my lovely wife now."

Allister turned. The woman coming toward him was not the teenager he'd seen all those years ago. Pictures, the few that he'd been able to get of her, did not do her justice. Christ, she looked just like her mother, including the glint of hatred that was shining in her eyes.

"Father." He nodded, not even sure how to address this person she'd become. He knew that it was stupid to have thought of her as his child, weak with her love for him. But now he could see that not only had he been mistaken about how she'd matured over the years, but the love that she'd had for him was completely gone from her heart. "I see you've been getting to know my husband. It's really too bad that you're not going to be around long enough to get to really know him. But you should know that he's nothing like you. Which I must say I find to be very refreshing."

"You're coming home with me, Dillon. I don't care what you think you've been up to, but I want you home. I told you when you were younger that I owned you and you were mine. See that you don't forget that." She laughed, and Allister had had enough. He drew back his hand to hit her when his arm was suddenly behind his back and up near his shoulders. He heard his wrist break just before the pain took his breath away.

"Touch her and I will kill you." Not a threat. This was a full promise from the man that held him. And Allister knew that Landon would do just what he said. "I'm going to let you go now, and you're going to tell her you're sorry."

"Sorry for what?" His arm was jerked up higher and Allister wanted to puke, the pain was so bad. "Christ, you motherfucker...yes, I'm sorry. Sorry I ever had her."

Allister never knew what happened after that, the pain took him away. Not only that, but he was pretty sure that he pissed himself while he was at it. The darkness just reached up and bitch slapped him into another realm.

When he woke up, he was in the emergency room at a hospital, and he was strapped to the bed. He was afraid it was a handcuff, but it was only a leather strap and his relief was profound. He had an IV in the back of his other hand that didn't bother him overly much, as he knew how to deal with that as well. A man was sitting in the chair next to his bed, and he watched him as he looked at the file on his lap. When he looked up, Allister knew the real meaning of fear.

"Allister Payton Malone?" Allister nodded before he could think that he shouldn't. "I'm Agent Theodore Drake of the Federal Bureau of Investigations. I'm here to speak to you about some unsolved murders."

"I want my lawyer." Drake nodded and stood up. That was when Allister noticed that there were others in the room with them. Men in suits as well as uniforms. And those men had on bullet proof vests, all of them strapped tightly to their chests. But it was the guns across their chests that had him swallowing hard and thinking harder. "What's this really about? Did someone turn me in for something I didn't do?"

"I doubt very much you really expect me to answer that, do you? You've already lawyered up, right? And even if I were inclined to do so, you'd not like the answer any more than I would." At his nod, two men came up and read him his rights as they cuffed not only his hand to the bed, but both his ankles as well. He was well and truly fucked right now. "Mr. Malone, until such time that you can be moved to a facility to keep you safe, you will have guards on you at all times. And if you should decide to talk, these gentlemen here know how to reach me."

The man was leaving him. "Hey? Wait a minute. You can't do this. Whatever you think you have on me, you're dead wrong. I'm here visiting my daughter. And her new husband. Landon Logan."

"Yeah? I heard about that visit too. Didn't go as well as you hoped, did it?" Drake smiled at him. "I'll be around if you want to talk, Malone. But if I were you, I'd get my ducks all lined up first. I don't think this is going to go any better than it did at the antique shop."

Allister lay there for a good hour trying to think what the fuck just happened to him. He'd been on a mission, yes, but for it to end up where he was in trouble with the Feds was not something that would have ever have occurred to him. His daughter was going to have to pay for this shit. He didn't have time for her stupidity. Allister asked for and received a phone.

After talking to his attorney for ten minutes, telling him he was being held, the man said he'd take care of things on this end. It was what he paid the man for so he'd better, Allister told him. As he made arrangements to come to him, Allister thought of the plan that he'd set up all those years ago with the man, and told him that it was time. Nothing more, just that it was time.

There was a long pause. Both of them knew that the line was being listened in on before Garrett finally spoke. "I'll have it taken care of as well. I will see you in the morning. In the meantime, please keep your mouth shut and don't ask them questions. Anything and everything will be recorded."

"Yes. I'm aware of that." After he handed the phone back to one of the men guarding him, he lay back. Things were about to get very bad for his daughter. He knew that she'd be dead before Garrett landed in this godforsaken shit hole.

It was, as far as Allister was concerned, no less than she deserved after all the misery she'd put him through.

CHAPTER 9

Dillon was stunned. Not just that, but she was pretty sure that this was all a joke. A terrible one, but a joke all the same. She looked at Landon when he said her name, she was sure for the second or third time.

"Are you all right?" She nodded, then shook her head. "Yeah, I'm right there with you. I had Hugh check it three times and for Billy to go and see as well. It's all true."

"But why?" He shrugged and told her that someone else was looking into everything that might give them solid answers. "I need to...I have to say this out loud. I think...I need to say it so I can believe this. That day...you went to your parents' that day to find out what they wanted, and found out that they wanted you to marry some woman. A woman that would seal the deal on something that they had set up before you got there. You met me and we married. Now we find out that it was their plan all along. That your parents and my father had worked it out that we'd marry. And that a merger, I think you called it, would make their lives a good deal better. And in the end, we'd be dead."

"Yeah. All that in just six months after the wedding too. They had it planned, right to the second, that while honeymooning in some other country, our plane would go down making both of them very rich. The policy that Grandda found has you listed as my wife, and that my parents and your father are sole benefactors. The date of our wedding, however, is two months from now; the plane tickets already bought, and have been for several weeks. According to the wedding invitations that are being put together right now, your father is giving you away and my parents are having this huge fucking dinner party the night before. They can plan, I'll give them that. Oh, and Mother has an entire staff working on the invitations to get them ready to go out on Friday."

"This is insane." He agreed with her. "How the fuck do they even know each other? And worse yet, how the hell did they think they were going to pull this off if neither of us knew each other?"

Hugh sat down at the table with them and handed her a sheet of paper. She laid it down without reading it. Hugh looked at him and explained. This was becoming more and more surreal with each minute.

"The two of you don't have to be present to make this look good. In fact, I'm pretty sure that's what they planned too. No one has seen either of you for years, and from what I've heard, most people had no idea that Dillon was even a female. The invitations are going out now, and as soon as your *pictures* hit the papers, everyone will think that the couple that was paid to do this is actually you guys." Landon picked up the paper and read it to her. "Yeah, I thought the fact that you two met years ago was stretching it a little, but who knows what the hell these people are capable of?"

"Murder. And apparently insurance fraud. Who would sell them a policy on two people that aren't married? Not to mention, why do they get to do this anyway? Shouldn't we have some say in who gets our money when we die?" Hugh told her that he could take out a policy on them and they'd never know. "So just anyone can collect on perfect strangers?"

"Pretty much. Haven't you heard of those funding sites were someone will set one up for this needy person for one reason or another and collect on it when the goal is hit? Happens more than people realize." Hugh told her he was sorry about this. "But on the other side of this, if something does happen to you, they get double the insurance money."

"Not funny, jerk off." Hugh left them after Landon cuffed him hard on the shoulder. This really wasn't funny. None of it was. "Honey, we'll be all right. I have my attorney looking into some things too. Your father and my parents are going to be in deep shit when this hits the fan."

"You said that before. All I can see is that they're profiting off of things that they have no rights to, making our lives a living hell, and all they're doing is sitting in their nice comfy home with dead bodies floating around. Did I miss something?" Landon answered her. "Oh, yeah, let us not forget that my father is going to prison for a very long time if not forever, yet he looks and acts like a man without a care in the world."

"He won't last a week in prison." She shivered when she realized what he meant. Her father had made some very big enemies, both on this side of the living and the other. She wondered how they would make it work, him being on the inside and them...well, ghosts. She looked up at Landon when he said that Billy wanted to ask her some things.

"He said that there is a friend of his that needs your help. The little girl has been taken from her mother and he knows that she's still alive and well, but the father is a known drug addict, and while he wouldn't hurt the child normally, he might get high and forget about her." Nodding, she asked him who it was. "He said to tell you that she'll be here soon. Teddy has told her of us."

"I see. And this mom, is she any better than the man that took her?" Dillon told Billy she was sorry. "I have a very jaded view of people right now. I mean, who does this to a child that they created?"

"He said that she's a good woman, her mother is...living with her to keep her safe, and Billy and she have been friends for some time. He said that he wouldn't ask, but he can't stand to see either of them hurting like this." The doorbell sounded just as she was going to tell him she would do it. And before she could remember that there was someone in the house to answer the door, she stood up. Something touched her just as she was taking a step.

"Landon?" He said he was there. "Something...someone is here. With me. I can feel them but...but I can't see them."

"I've never seen her before either. She's nodding to me. I don't think she can speak to us." Dillon nodded, but knew that the woman, like the things she touched to find someone, could tell her in ways that others might not know. "She's been killed."

"Yes. I know." The touch moved over her face, like fingers running down her cheek. While she couldn't actually see her, she could see her memories like her own. "She's been killed by my father. He murdered her three months ago when he found her spying on him. She works for the police...no, not the police, but the Feds."

"Does she know that she's dead?" Dillon didn't know how to ask her questions, but she seemed to understand Landon. She told him that she did. "Does she know where she is? Buried, I mean?"

"Yes. She is in a landfill about four miles from my father's home. A man by the name of Jamie Winter took her there. He was on her list of known suspects when she was put undercover in the house. She wants you to call her handler and let him know where she is." Landon asked her for that name. "I'm sorry, she doesn't remember. Her name either. Is that right?"

"Sometimes. There have been times when we've been on cases where the people had no idea they were gone, only that they were lost. Others can tell you everything about themselves, but not their name. It's sad." The woman agreed with him. "Ask her if I may contact Teddy Drake?"

"She said to tell you that you can talk to her, but she cannot answer you for some reason. Can you...is it possible that you can see why she can't answer on her own?" He said that he could, but didn't elaborate. "I see. I don't want to know, do I?"

"No, sweetheart, you don't." He asked her two more questions just as Moses, husband to their cook Alice Walker, and a cook too, came into the room telling them that they had a visitor. Landon asked to have her put in the other room and Moses just stood there. "Is there something wrong?"

"I can see the light, sir. I could always see some people's life force if it was strong, but right now, Mrs. Landon is glowing with it. Is she like you and the others?"

"Something like us, but she can do things we can't." Moses nodded. "Can you speak or see the dead, Moses?"

"No sir. I can see the light, that's all. And not on the dead. If I could, I'd have me a conversation with a few of them. But just the living." Landon laughed when Moses did. "I'll have tea brought in too. Alice told me how to do it. The young miss looks all done in. And if you want to know, her light is blue, sad blue."

After giving Landon as much information as she could get from the woman, including where she thought her apartment was, Dillon went to the parlor just as Moses was rolling in a tea cart. Dillon asked Moses if it was part of the house or did they buy it the other day. She'd gotten so many things that she couldn't remember any more.

"The shop, mistress. Mrs. Vinnie said it would be proper to have it. It's very nice not to have to carry a tray, I'll have to say." She agreed with him and stood by the door with him until he smiled at her. "You can't help her if you don't go in. My missus said to tell you that she'll bake you a bunch of those chocolate chip cookies if you do this."

Nodding and asking him to please call the police for her, she moved into the room. The woman standing there was distraught, and if the tissue in her hand, torn and shredded, was any indication, she was crying a good deal as well. Dillon introduced herself to her as Kerrie, the only name she used when she was working.

"I just don't know what to do now. He has taken her before, but the police were able to get him before he got too far. This time I think he had help. Benny doesn't drive, you see, and had...he actually took my daughter and tried to escape with a bike the last time. He's not overly bright." Dillon nodded and handed her a box of tissues. "He was a stalker, you see. Followed me everywhere all the time. Then one night he...he took me in the parking lot where I worked. Raped me and left me there for anyone to come along and kill me. But by the grace of God, someone took me to the hospital. It wasn't until weeks later that I found out that I had conceived. It was a hard decision to make to keep her, but she's the best thing that has ever happened to me in all my life. I love her so much."

"I don't know, darling, I really don't. But we're going to get her back. I promise you." She nodded and let him hold her. "I have Garth and Grandma looking for Dillon. They're going to stay with her. Let me go and I'll see if I can find Landon. Hopefully she took him with her."

Landon hadn't gone and he had no idea where Dillon was either. Garth said he was still looking and had some of his crew helping, and Connie was so upset over the baby that she was having a hard time staying focused. Billy was moving back and forth between where they were and their daughter was so much that it was weakening him. Kari asked him to stay with Aster and help her.

"I feel useless is what I am." She assured him that knowing that her daughter was in good hands was all that was keeping her sane right now. "Aster is watching over her like it was her own. Talking to her, telling her to be quiet so as not to piss off that man. He's a calm one, that man is. Like he's done this before. Can't find a thing on him just now, but I will, you can bet on that."

When the house phone rang some two hours later, the house was filled with people. There were agents that were standing around asking the same questions over and over, and cops, all of them just as anxious as they were, waiting for the first clue. Steele answered the phone and handed it to her after saying hello.

"It's Dillon. I don't have time to talk. But you can find her. Just use that incredible talent of yours." Kari asked her where she was just as Aster appeared in the room. "She's just fine now. I had him...I'm sorry about this, Kari. I never meant for this to happen to you. Tell Landon...tell him that I love him with all of my heart, and I'm so very sorry we didn't get to go shopping like he wanted."

Then the line was dead. Kari looked up at Aster and asked her where the baby was. She knew there was some sort of clue in what Dillon was saying to her, but for now all she could think about was her child.

"I can't take you there, but she's not with the man any longer. Dillon had him put her along the side of the road, and I made Billy and Carlton stay with her so I could come back to speak to you. Then Dillon and that man drove off together." Aster looked at Landon. "She's hurt. He hit her. And she's been shot. I'm not really sure how it happened as I was with the baby, but she's losing blood."

"Where did they go?" Aster told Landon she could show him the direction they took when they got to the baby. "Where?"

"I don't know. I'm so sorry, but I have no sense of direction. I just don't know." Aster looked at her. "You can find her, right? Don't you have a connection with her? Like you do with my brother?"

"I do." Kari stood up. "I can find her." Kari moved out of the room with Steele right behind her. She knew there was no point in asking him to stay behind. Stripping off her shirt and bra as soon as she entered the office, she looked at him. "I can find her as my panther. She can call to me. What I want you to do is find Dillon. She saved our daughter's life, and I can only do the same for her. And I have a message from her for Landon. I'm not sure what it means, but tell him they didn't get to go shopping like he wanted and that she loves him very much."

"Do you know what that means?" Kari said that she didn't and let her panther take her. "When this is done, you and I are going to go back out into the woods and I'm going to let you run me down, all right?"

Yes. More than all right. When I come back, you had better have some progress in getting my friend back, do you understand me? He smiled at her and nodded. *Good. I'll let you know when I have her. You'll have to bring me clothing, all right?*

"Yes. But please be careful. I can't lose you. I love you." Kari told him that she loved him as well and moved out the door that he held open for her. "I'll let you know when I find things out."

Kari moved across the yard, thankful for the first time in her life that someone had converted her to a panther without her permission. Calling out to her daughter, she told her that she was coming and sent her all her love. Kari nearly fell over the log she was moving over when the love that she sent her was returned. Kari was so happy she nearly forgot to tell Steele that she was going to find her. That their child would be home soon.

CHAPTER 10

Dillon moved as best she could without pissing off the man who had her by the hair. She was in a great deal of pain, but she was sure that the baby was safe and that was enough for her. Garrett, her father's attorney and number one thug, had dragged her down the hallway until she wanted to kill him. She might just yet, she thought with a grin. It was short lived when the door opened in front of her and she was thrown in. The door slammed shut behind her, and she just sat there. He looked at her through an opening in the door, and she wanted to get up and slap the smile off his face before he spoke to her.

"Your daddy will be here as soon as his bail money is approved. And when he gets here, I wouldn't expect him to welcome you back into his life with open arms." She didn't say anything, thinking to save her energy for more important things, like killing them both. "Oh, and your in-laws are on their way in too. They have a few words to say to you as well."

"I'm sure they do." Dillon moved to the wall to lean against it and to watch the door. She had no idea what she would do if they came into this room with her to cause her any harm, but she was going to be able to look them in the eye. When the shadows moved in front of her, she nearly screamed, but didn't when she saw who was standing there.

"Vinnie. How the hell did you find me?" She sat down on the floor but didn't come any closer. When she put her finger to her mouth for her to be quiet, Dillon closed her mouth to the million and one questions that were popping up at random. The scuffle at the door had her looking up. When the door opened, she had to fight hard not to cringe from the couple standing there.

"Mother fuck. Your father said we'd be surprised when we saw you. Right under our fucking noses all the time. And to think that you went and made our son do what we wanted anyway. That is just about the best news I've heard in some time." Dillon stared at the man in front of her, and then at the woman when she entered the small cell as well. Landon's parents were mean spirited as they came. "Where is he? We need you to bring Landon here right now so we can end this."

Dillon laughed at the man. "Let me see if I can pull him out of my ass for you. Or call him. I'm sure that I can use my cell phone to...oops. The idiot that shot me took it from me." The man looked at her oddly before she continued. "Where the hell was I supposed to put him? Not to mention, I was told to come alone. Alone does not mean I bring my husband with me."

Dillon looked at Vinnie when she laughed, but neither of the Logans did. They couldn't see her. And when Mr. Logan stepped on Vinnie's outstretched leg, Dillon knew that she was right. Then Vinnie spoke to her in a normal calm voice that did wonders to her own set of nerves.

Now that you've figured it out, I want you to know that I can't help you until we know what the plan is. I want to. Nothing would make me feel better than to tear their throats out and let them bleed to death right here in this room. But the police, in all their wisdom, won't like that overly much. Dillon said nothing. *We know where you are. Well, I do. And a few other people. Steele does, but we've not told Landon. I think it would be a mistake to have him come in here to rescue you just now.*

Nodding quickly, Dillon watched the couple. She thought perhaps they were waiting for her to answer them, but for the life of her, she had no idea what they might have said. Not that she cared. She wasn't going to bring Landon here for them to kill him.

"You two are pretty stupid if you've hooked up with my father." Mr. Logan snorted at her and Mrs. Logan asked her why she thought that. "He's a criminal. Well, I guess that's sort of like calling the kettle black, isn't it? You two have more ghosts in your wake than most cemeteries, don't you?"

"It was do or die, young lady, and we decided that we enjoy the lifestyle that we have now." She remembered the paperwork that she'd picked up from Earl that day. And wondered if it had been filed yet. She just shook her head and laughed at them.

"You mean your father's money? I hate to tell you this, buddy, but that's about to go up in smoke too. Did you really think that no one would find the will? I mean, holy Christ, Landon told you that he talked to his grandda all the time. Didn't you think he'd let him know where the original was?" Mrs. Logan stiffened at her words and looked at her husband. There was worry there, and Dillon was glad for it. "You two won't be able to profit off the insurance you've taken out on Landon or me either. Not with the way things are going for you. Landon and I have already filed our marriage license, so the one you have dated before the wedding is void. Insurance fraud is going to bite you in the ass."

"What do you mean about my father's will? No one has seen that since the old bastard died." Dillon said that she and Landon had taken it to the courthouse several days ago. Right after Grandda had told her where to find it. "No. You can't have."

"Why do people keep saying that to us? We *can* have done it, you moron. And furthermore, we're going to stay right here on the ground when we go on our honeymoon, too. No plane crashes for you to collect on." He started for her, but she brought him up short with her next words. "You do, and I swear to Christ you'll never know what hit you. I'll have you dead before your heart beats again."

"Landy, what's she saying? I thought you said that you took care of that will. That no one would ever find it." Mr. Logan told her to shut up. He had it worked out. "How? If he's filed his paperwork, then the insurance is not going to pay off. And I'm not going to go to jail for this. You told me that you had it all taken care of. Am I to assume that my father's will is out there somewhere as well?"

"No. I'm pretty sure that you're going to jail for murder as well as a lot of other things. Why the hell did you keep the hearts of the people you killed in the armor in your living room?" Mr. Logan came toward her this time and kicked her in the head. Dizziness swamped her, but she stopped Vinnie from leaving her to get the police by raising her hand. "You thinking of adding me to your collection? I'd seriously reconsider that. I'm not an old man with a baby in my arms."

He laughed; threw back his head and laughed. Then, when Mr. Logan leaned against the wall drawing a gun, Dillon thought for sure that he was going to finish her off. She wasn't sure how much more she could take.

"Since I know for a fact that you're never leaving this room on your own, I'll tell you. The hearts? Well, those are of the two people in the world who stood in our way. Her father and mine. They had it in their heads that we weren't nice people and were going to turn us in. Not even having Landon, their pride and joy, could keep my nosey father out of our business, so I killed him while he sat in our living room holding my son." Dillon wondered if Landon's grandda knew this and was pretty sure he did. It explained why the man had watched over his grandson so well. He was protecting him from his parents. Dillon asked about the other heart. Mrs. Logan laughed.

"My daddy. He was going to change his will. Told me that he was disappointed in me. I cannot tell you how disappointing he was to me, with his rules and ways of doing things. Never a nice word to say about how much money we were raking in. Never once told me how my house was bigger than his. You should have seen him when I had him in the pool. Begging me to let him get out. Telling me how tired he was. Every time he tried, I'd shoot toward him. Never at him, but he didn't have to know that. And once he was just too tired to get out, I watched him drown where he was. Getting his heart from him was a little trickier, but with the kind of money I was going to be making from his death, I could have anything I wanted."

"You people are sick fucks." The blow to her head this time was nothing she could have avoided. Nor could she hold onto her consciousness. It was as if the lights were turned off and she was plunged into total darkness.

~~~

Landon stood where they told him to and didn't move. He was going to hit someone if they didn't give him any

151

information, and the longer he stood there, waiting, the more people were going to be killed when he was released.

"You keep looking like that and nobody is going to come to you when they've processed the scene." Landon glared at his grandda, who only laughed. "She's pretty pissed off herself, so you know. Her temper is going to be legendary when they get her loaded up on that bed."

"Is she all right?" Grandda said she was hurt, bleeding, but was gonna make it. "I need to see her. Can't they see what it's doing to me to not be able to see her?"

"They can. But it's more important that they get this right the first time. There won't be any going back if they mess up. And I, for one, want those two behind bars for the rest of their days." Landon nodded, but he didn't have to like it.

Just over an hour ago, the police had stormed the warehouse he'd led them to. He and Dillon had been talking about going shopping, when they were done for the day, at Mitch and Vinnie's warehouse. There were some things, bedroom furniture, that they were still missing, and Vinnie told them there was a lot of that sort of stuff they'd not had any time to inventory just yet. He knew when he got the message from Steele where she was going.

"Vinnie said that they murdered you." That had nearly had him going to the cruiser where his parents were being held and killing them both. They had killed the man that had come to mean more to him than they ever had. "I'm so sorry about that, Grandda. I wish I had known."

"No. It's better this way for all of us. Had you known, I think they would have killed you long before you were sent away to school. Took me a long time to convince them that they needed you out of the house before they did it. I know that you were lonely, son, but it was the only way I knew to keep you safe." Landon nodded. He knew that now. "They're going to find what is left of my body soon. I'd like you to bury it out with your grandmother. They went and took my body off and had me buried in a plot far away from here. I see her once in a while, but not nearly as much as I'd like to."

"I can do that for you. No problem." Grandda nodded, and Landon felt better now. Less murderous. At least for the moment.

When the police came out of the building, Landon made his way to the entrance just as the ambulance backed to where they were. They were being extra cautious right now because Allister was on the loose. No one had realized he wasn't in his room until about an hour ago.

"Hello." Landon reached out to touch Dillon's hand that was wrapped up in a gauze when he saw her. "Your father hit me."

"I can see that. I hope you got in a few punches of your own." She shook her head, then moaned. "Just rest, honey. Don't move. I'm going to follow you in my truck, as they won't let me ride with you. The police can do a better job than I can in protecting you."

"Vinnie saved my life." He knew that as well. Vinnie had told him what had happened and what his parents had said. He owed her more than he could ever repay. "When he kicked me, I thought for sure she was going to kill him. But she wasn't really there, was she?"

"No. She wanted to go to you, but it was too dangerous for her. But she said that you were strong and that you kept them talking until the police arrived. Which I find hard to believe. Usually they just never shut up." She laughed, then winced at the pain of it. "I'm going to let them take you in now. Steele said he'd drive me."

"Good." When she laid her head back, he knew she had to get going. Grandda had told him that she had a broken wrist, as well as a concussion. She was going to be all right, but it was going to take a little while to mend. She'd lost a lot of blood when she was shot, too. "Landon? When we get home, do you think I can just lay around for a couple of days? I'm very tired of all this stress we've been dealing with lately."

"I am as well, love. And I'm making arrangements for you to have a nice long rest in one of my homes. You'll love it. People to wait on you hand and foot while you do nothing but rest up." She smiled at him just as her hand in his went limp. The meds that they'd given her had finally kicked in fully.

By the time they made it to the hospital, she was in surgery. Landon sat in the waiting room as several of the same police officers moved about. Each of them had on heavy jackets and were armed as well. None of them looked like they were going to rest easy so long as they were needed. Landon leaned back in his seat and closed his eyes.

His parents had murdered his grandda. While in the back of his mind he knew that it was true, it was still hard for him to wrap his mind around. Ever since Grandda had started to hang around him, he'd told Landon that he'd been dead before he was born. Now he knew the real story.

"He left you everything." Lee Vargas, his attorney, had come to him just after he'd turned all the paperwork over to him that Dillon had picked up. Landon had never bothered reading it. He didn't remember why right now, but there had been so much going on that he'd just called Lee and told him that he was giving it to him. "The house, the money. Even his collection of cars, in the hopes that someday you'd run over your father with one of them. It was right there in the will too."

They both laughed over that. Landon watched his grandda as he sat in the room with the two of them. Lee went on to tell him of the provisions that had been made for him, even when he was supposed to get his money from the estate. His parents had been given a house, according to his grandda's will—not the one that they lived in—as well as a yearly check that was to help with their expenses.

"It wasn't much of a house. Two bedrooms, and a bath. Nothing like the one that they live in now. And when it comes time for them to be moved out and into a nice cell in prison, which I'm assuming you will want, all the things that are in the house stay. They can't even take their clothing with them because they had knowledge of this will." Landon had asked him how he knew that. "Your father and mother both signed it. On each page at the bottom, so that there would be no problems later, the will stated who got what. I looked it up. You were about twenty-four hours old when the will was updated with your name in the place of baby Logan."

Someone touched his arm, and he sat up on the seat to talk to the man. Steele was his best friend. He was sure that he was to the others, too. But to Landon, he would forever be the one person that he would go to when he needed someone to talk to. Steele asked him if he was all right.

"Yes. I think so. They told me she'd be in surgery for about an hour or two. Then they'd move her to recovery where I can see her. She's been beat up pretty badly." Steele said he'd seen her too. "My father murdered Grandda."

"I heard. I'm so sorry about that. You and I, we sure did win the lottery when it came to parents." Landon told him he thought they all had. "No kidding. You think that was what made us what we are? I mean, not necromancers, but hard men?"

"Hard? We're hardly what I would consider hard now, would you? I mean, I've seen you around Kari. And when Aster is in your arms, you look like day old ice cream. A puddle of mush." Steele told him to wait until he had his own children. "We're going to adopt. I mean, we'll have our own children too, but we're going to take in a couple of kids that have nowhere else to go for now. Billy is looking to see if he can find a child like us, one that might be alone too."

"Kari and I are going to as well when Aster is a little older. I think Mitch and Vinnie are working to that end as well." Nick had just announced that morning that Addie was going to have a baby, so he knew that they were going to wait to adopt. Each of them had a lot to offer a child, and more if the kid was anything like they were. "I have a favor to ask you. As soon as you can leave here knowing that Dillon is going to be all right. It's about Vinnie's father. I need help dealing with him."

"You know that I will do whatever you need of me." Steele said he appreciated that. "What is it we're going to be doing? I'm assuming it's to send him to hell."

"Something like that. I've been trying to think how to do this without having a mess on my hands. As you know, Horatio hasn't been able to go back to his place of death. So the last I heard he's been taking over the bodies of the living and using them to kill. Last weekend he took the body of an elderly man in a nursing home and tried to get him to kill all the residents there. Kari and I think he's trying to gather him an army again." Landon asked him what had happened. "The man had no gun, of course, and the only weapon he had at his disposal was a small butter knife. He caused himself more harm than he did anyone else, but it was enough to have me called in. The poor man kept saying that he'd been possessed. Of course he had, but not by a demon."

"What's the plan then? You have one, right?" Steele said that he had, but he was going to need his help to pull it off. "Like I said, I'll do whatever you need."

The doctor came down the hall toward them and both he and Steele stood up. Kari was at home with the baby and the rest of the men were with them. With Allister out, no one was safe just yet. The doctor asked them if one of them was Dillon's husband.

"I am, but he stays too please. I need him here." The doctor sat down and smiled. Immediately he felt much better. "She's going to be all right then."

"Oh yes. She's going to be just fine. I want to wait a few days before I send her home, much to her displeasure. She's quite a woman, that wife of yours." Landon asked him what she'd done. "Almost as soon as the IV keeping her under was shut off, she came awake cursing like a sailor and telling the nurses to get you. She said that she was going to bring a shit storm down on me so hard that I'd be feeling it for weeks. I came here when she threatened my manhood. Again."

Landon laughed, as did Steele. He could not wait to get her home, where he could show her just how much he loved her.

It was another hour before he got to go back and see her. She was doing fine, but they didn't want her to get an infection this late in the game. As he was told not to touch any of the bandages on her face or hands, he thought about the first thing he was going to say to her. Kissing her, he'd been told, was going to be next to impossible with all the bruising. But he was going to make it work if he had to hurt himself to do it. As soon as he entered the room, however, all he could do was sob and look at her.

"I could kill him." Dillon told him it wasn't that bad. He knew better…he could see what had been done to her. He'd seen her earlier, of course, but the swelling hadn't started as yet, she had had blood and bandages on her face, and her hands had been covered by the blanket they had on her.

Her cheek was still bandaged with a large gauze, and he'd been told she had seventeen stitches in it. Her nose had been broken, and both her eyes were nearly swollen shut. There were stitches in her left brow as well as along her chin. He touched his fingers to hers and saw that her wrist was in a thick cast, and the other was wrapped up on a board to keep it still while the IV was running. Landon leaned in and kissed her gently on her lip, the one that was showing, and held her while they both fought more tears.

"She has four broken ribs as well as a sprained knee. All of which will heal nicely. The gunshot wound is clean and stitched up, and the loss of blood is a little concerning, but not so long as she keeps getting fluids like she is." Landon nodded, unable to speak to the doctor as he rattled off what had happened to Dillon, as well as what he'd done to repair it. "Her lungs are clear, which is amazing since I fully expected them to be damaged as well. And her fingers, only one is broken. There doesn't seem to be any permanent damage done to her. We're going to keep her here for a few more days, just in the event that her lungs fill with fluid and we need to operate again. But in a few days, a week at the most, you can take her home."

After the doctor left them, Landon watched Dillon drift in and out of sleep. She was all he had in the world right now, and he didn't want anything else to happen to her. When the nurse came in a few minutes later and said that she needed to take Dillon's blood pressure, Landon nearly laughed as it became evident she didn't even know where to start.

He never left her. Not that he would have if they made him, but he slept in the chair while she rested. When morning came and he was asked to step out so they could change the bandages, he told them that when she came home he was going to need to know how to do it and wished to stay. Ten minutes later a nurse was not only showing him how to take the old dressing off, but how to put it back on so that there wouldn't be any marks to her skin. He was shaking when she was finished, and wished that he could have had a little of the pain meds she was getting after they left them alone. Landon knew it was going to be a long time before he let her out of his sight again.

CHAPTER 11

Allister was just sitting down to dinner when his butler came into the room. His face might have been comical if he wasn't so sure that he was afraid. Asking him what was wrong only got the man to babbling and finally, Allister got up to see what the problem was. He didn't have any idea who the woman was that stood there on his doorstep.

"Invite me in." He backed from her. But when she repeated herself, he felt as if he had no choice whatsoever but to do as she wanted. As soon as she was in the room with him, Allister knew that he'd made the biggest mistake of his life. She rushed him until she was standing there holding him above the floor with one hand.

He struggled for a few seconds until he remembered that he was armed. Reaching into his pocket for his gun, he nearly had it pointed at her when she smiled at him. Allister felt his bladder just let go. The women had long, sharp fangs.

"Shooting me will only piss me off. And I think we've had enough piss for one day, don't you?" He nodded. "Now. I'm going to put you down and if you try to run, you're going to ruin all my fun. And that will be terrible for me. It matters little to you, because either way, you're a dead man."

As soon as his feet touched the floor he felt his knees nearly buckle. But she picked him up again and sat him down on the couch. He never realized that they'd left the front hall and were now in his office. She sat down at his desk, and he didn't have the energy to tell her to get away. Terror was making him weak. And weak minded. But he soon recovered when she began going through his drawers.

"What do you want? Whatever it is, you can just forget it. I'm not going to be playing whatever games you have in mind." She grinned again. "What do you think you're going to do? Kill me like you said? No, you won't. I'm a very powerful man."

"You're a fool if you think I'm going to let you go. You are going to die. By my hand. But before you do, you're going to do a few things for me." He told her to fuck off. "Bad manners will not make your death a quick one, Allister. It will only make me have more fun while I kill you."

"Who are you? And why do you think you have any rights to kill me?" She told him her name. "Means nothing to me. I don't know a Vinnie Riley, and if you think those fake teeth are going to scare me, you're stupider than I think you are. I have men all over this place that will come to me with just a shout."

"They're dead. All of them. Go ahead, call out to them. See if anyone comes. Oh, and the butler you have here, as well as the cook, they're gone. I sent them on their way after you allowed me to come in." She tisked at him. "Bad news on that. If you had not let me in, you might have lived a little while longer. Now I have you all to myself."

He was beginning to think she wasn't lying to him. But just to be sure, he called out to his body guards. All three of them. No one came, and when she got up to go to the door, he thought perhaps she was going to show him where they were. She did, but it wasn't to see his men tied up.

They were indeed dead. Victor's head was nowhere near his body, and the other two men had had their throats torn out. Not cut...no, they were simply torn out, like an animal had bitten down on them and just ripped. He looked at Vinnie when she said his name.

"You're going to make a hasty will, leaving all your belongings to your lovely daughter. Also, I have a list of people here I want you to confess to killing." He took the paper with at least three dozen names on it. "I know there are more, names I mean, but this will do for now. The rest will, I'm sure, come forward after you're gone. You have a nice welcoming party just waiting for you to draw your last breath."

"What do you mean?" He put the paper in his lap, not at all caring for the way it shook in his hand. "You must think I'm a sap if you believe I'm going to leave shit to my daughter. She'll be dead soon enough anyway. And when she is, I'm going to go and piss on her grave."

Vinnie looked at his lap and laughed. "You might want to clean up a bit if you really think that's ever going to happen. And as for your welcoming party? Well, it's the people on that list. The ones that you murdered. Oh, and the man you sent to kill Dillon and her husband is in police care. You should really do a better job of checking out your employees before you pay them two million dollars for a job that was never going to happen. He worked for the Feds and is telling them all about you right about now."

"No." She nodded and told him to go to the desk. It was as if he had no control over his body. He was standing up and moving to the desk before she sat down on the chair across from him...not the couch he'd been in. He noticed as it was stained wet with his urine. "What are you doing to me? You're doing this, aren't you?"

"I am. Now reach into your top left drawer and pull out the legal pad that's there." He did this, his hands not listening to him as he tried to tell himself not to do it. "I'm telling you right now, this is much easier than I thought it would be. I thought that you'd be harder to control. I guess it goes to show you that you can't judge a book by its cover."

Allister wrote what she told him to. Each word was as hard as the next. He not only left his daughter his vast collection of paintings, but told her in the letter where each of his holdings were, and his homes, even the ones that were worth no more than the paper he was writing on.

By the time he was told he was finished, Allister was beyond exhausted. Fighting the woman had taken its toll on him. But every word she said, every command that she'd given him, he'd done it without being able to fight her off.

"Now what? You think that anyone will believe that I did this on my own? I have news for you, no one will take this seriously. They know me better that that." She said she had that covered too. With a snap of her fingers, a man entered the room, stepping over the bodies as if they weren't there.

"This is my attorney. He's used to doing things that are slightly unconventional. And when I ask him to do something, not demand as I have you, then I know it will be done properly." Before he could say a word, he was signing another form stating that he'd written the will he'd just made of his own free will.

"It'll never stand up in court. No one will go against me when I tell them what you've done to me today." She said nothing and just watched him. It was unnerving having her stare at him like she was, and he felt himself squirm in his seat. "Who sent you?"

"No one. I came here all on my own. You see, I really have come to love Dillon. She's nothing like you, thankfully, and I want her to have this all behind her while she and Landon make a life together. I talked it over with Steele, and we decided that you need to be dead." He thought her mad and said so. "No, at least not in the way you're thinking. I am mad, but at you, not in the head. Now. Write out the confession."

Again he had no way of not doing as she said. Each name he wrote, she told him that they were there to collect. Collect what, he asked her several times, but she only gave him the next name on the list until all of them were written down, with where the body was buried written right next to it. If anyone got a hold of this, he was going to prison for a very long time.

After he was finished with it, she had him put it in the envelope that she had on her and seal it with his own tongue. He never did this, never put his DNA out where it could be used against him, and marveled at how easily she'd made him do that as well. To do so now made him realize what sort of control she had over him. As the envelope was put on his desk and his pens put away, he asked her what the fuck she thought was going to happen now.

"You're going to die." She stood up then, moving toward him with a slow gait that made him think of beautiful women on a runway. But she was deadly too. This woman would kill without a second's hesitation. He knew as surely as he was sitting there that he was going to die by her hand, just as she'd told him.

"I'll give you all my money." She laughed as she stood in front of him. "Everything is yours if you just leave here now."

"No." He watched in horror as she pulled out a gun and handed it to him. When she told him to put it to his chest, where his heart might have been, he could no more not do that than he could breathe. It occurred to him that there was going to be nothing he could give her to stop this madness just as she told him to pull the trigger. He did that as well, and felt the blast pierce his chest.

"Goodbye, Allister. I do hope you enjoy your afterlife. What little there will be in it for you." She sat down again then, not caring at all that he was dying right in front of her. As if she did it every day. For all he knew, she did. Allister felt his life draining away as he tried to stem the flow of blood coming from his chest.

He saw them then. The men and women that he'd killed. They faded into the room even as the blood pooled in his lap. Holding his chest did no good; he was bleeding to death as they stood there watching him. Then as his body slipped away, Dave Marshall, the first man he'd ever killed, slammed his fist into his face. Then the next man and the next, until he felt like he was broken.

"And tomorrow, they will begin again. Every day they'll come to you, Allister, forever and ever." She laughed then as she stood up. And when she walked out of the door and closed it softly behind her as he was beaten, Allister started to scream as they hurt him. Beaten by ghosts that he had killed.

~~~

Landon stood in the middle of the hall and just stared. He wasn't really sure what he was supposed to do or how to do anything. But his attorney had told him to meet him here and here he was. Earl handed him a thick chocolate chip cookie. Landon nearly sobbed when the thing seemed the only normal thing he'd seen for hours.

"You just walk around here and let me give you a tour. To have a man such as yourself here, no one knows what to think." Landon nodded, taking a bite out of the cookie as he moved with him. "How is the missus? I heard that she is doing much better now. Be on the mend soon, I'm told."

"Yes. She said to tell you that you're coming to live with us. If you want to, that is. She told me how kind you were to her." Earl stopped for just a second and Landon looked at him. "You don't have to, Earl. I know that you might have your heart set on retiring, and my house is much bigger but less work. We're not home much."

"I'd be honored, sir. You know...I was going to ask. I surely was. You've made my day, you have." They started toward the stairs again, to make their way to the bottom, Earl told him. "Are you taking any more of the staff? I should like to help you there. Not many would want to work for you. Not just you, but...well, sir, they rarely worked here when they didn't have to."

"You bring whomever you think. Like I said, it's a huge house." Earl said that he knew just the ones. "We have a cook, you know that, right? And her husband, Moses. He helps her there."

"Yes. We have met with Miss Izzy before. Your cook, Alice, she is a good woman. Miss Ruth, I believe she is setting to retire now. I don't think that your missus and Miss Ruth got along too well when she was here." Landon thought that was an understatement. Ruth didn't care for him overly much either. "It's best for all that she is retiring. Things will run smoothly without her around."

Landon agreed. As they moved from room to room, he thought about the items in the house. He had no attachments to any of it. There were some pictures of his grandparents that he took, a blanket that Grandda said he wanted, as well as a few things that had been his and Grandmas when they were owners of the house. A bedroom suite, as well as the silver picture frames with pictures of people that neither him nor Grandda knew. They were outside the room that he knew was his parents' when he looked at Earl.

"I can't." Earl seemed to understand and told him he'd take care of it. But Landon felt he needed to explain. "They were never much to me. I know that they're my parents and they really disliked me, but to go into their room and keep something from it? I can't do it. There is nothing in there that will mean any more to me than this house does."

The rest of the house was a blur. He kept the dining room table after it was approved by sending pictures of it to Dillon. He also kept the televisions. There were three in the lower levels alone that he thought would do well in the garage or basement of their house. Then there were the cars.

His grandda had collected them like some men did ties. He never drove them as far as anyone knew, and if he did, it was cleaned, waxed, and put back in the garage waiting for the next time he wanted to take one out for a bit of fun. As far as Landon knew, neither of his parents drove anywhere either that a limo couldn't convey them to just as easily, so he knew that they'd never touched them. He turned to Earl and offered him any of the cars he wanted.

"Oh no, sir. I could never do that." But he wanted it. The little red sports car that had been there since Landon had lived here as a child. "What will the others think?"

"I don't care. I'm going to sign it over to you." Earl looked at him, then at the car again. "Tomorrow. We'll go down and have the title turned over to your name in the morning. As for the rest...I think Steele wants to have a look at them, as well as Hugh. After they have their pick, then we might as well sell them off too."

The contents of the house that he didn't want were go be sold off at auction. There was already interest, and several people had asked him if he was going to sell. But Landon had an idea what he really wanted to do with it and the house, he just had to talk to him. He thought that the house and all the surrounding land would be perfect for Drew.

The man wasn't much of a social person, and this place was so far off the beaten path that it might be days before he saw anyone. There was plenty of room for him to spread out...a pool and pool house as well. Even the garage could be used for tinkering if he wanted. Landon was going to see if any of the other men in his family wanted to take one of the cars as well. He didn't care how much the estate was going to generate. As far as he was concerned it could rot to the ground. But this way, giving it away like he was going to do, would royally piss his father off. That made it worth it.

As Landon drove back to the hospital, he thought of where his parents had ended up. Both were in prison for the moment, awaiting their trials, and they'd both individually asked to see him. Steele and Hugh both told him he should go. Even Kari had told him that it wouldn't hurt him to see what they wanted, and he could have a good laugh when they asked him to bail them out.

"As of this morning you own it all. I had a judge look over the things that were left behind, and he made things move a little faster for you so you could sell them. He made me promise that you weren't going to use the money to get them a good attorney. I assured him that that wasn't even a question." Lee had come to see him at the house last night when he'd gone there to get some fresh clothing. "Even the houses that your father had on the market are now off, and in yours and Dillon's name. I've done the same for her father's things as well. Most of that is still in flux to see if there will be anyone coming back to sue him, but I don't foresee any problems. His estate is pretty vast, but no entanglements that I can see. The families that might want to sue him, they're going to be taken care of in the proper channels, but none of it will affect either of you."

"You think that his will, the one that they found with the body, it'll stand up?" Lee said that it would. His signature had been verified, as well as the items that had been listed on it were right where he said they'd be. "There is the matter of the stashes that he had. I'm having a few men that I trust go and get it. I'm glad that it was put in a separate paper so that you wouldn't get hit with taxes on it. That is a shit load of money all in cash."

Dillon's father was dead. His body had been found by his staff late last night. They thought he had killed his men, then written out a suicide note leaving everything to Dillon. Then a signed confession about the crimes he'd committed, as well as where to find the bodies. Telling Dillon had been the hardest thing he'd had to do in his life.

After Lee had left him, bringing him not just the news of the death of Allister but the rest of the paperwork that they'd have to sign off on, he went back to tell her. She had taken it very well, he'd thought, and then he told her of the will.

"He wouldn't have left me anything." He had to agree with her. The man hated her almost as much as his parents did him. "He might have left me an empty pop bottle or even a half-eaten sandwich, but not his estate. I don't know what happened, but he didn't do this."

"Lee said that everything was verified. Apparently he had a great many places that Lee thought were his run money. He accounted for that as well, and let you know where to find it. Lee is taking care of that as well." She nodded. "I'm going to sell my house to Drew if he wants it. I know that Hugh bought a house recently from Alexandra, so Drew is the only one that doesn't have his own place. And it's close to us. He's nearly our neighbor."

"I think that's a good idea. My father's house, the one here in town. What am I supposed to do with it?" He told her he had no idea, but whatever she wanted, he was okay with it. "I'd like to use it for something. Not a house. It's too...I don't know, too many terrible memories for me there. But we can think of something, right?"

"Yes. How about a hotel?" She asked him why that. "Last week when I was helping Vinnie move some of the antiques to the shop, she was saying that there just weren't enough places to stay in town, and that her buyers were coming from all over the world to look at the shop. I guess she had a lot of customers coming into town to visit and buy, and there is only the one hotel. We could convert it and use it that way. From what I understand there is already a bath for each bedroom, a huge kitchen, as well as a dining room. And the pool out back could help others unwind for the day. Vinnie might even let us fill it with her things with price tags on them."

They talked some more, Dillon suggesting that they open up the pool house as a secondary home for the staff. The thing was as big as a good-sized house, with three bedrooms and a nice deck that faced away from the house. It was on the table for now, something they could talk about later if they wanted.

171

Going through the lobby of the hospital, he picked up some flowers and a box of chocolates for them. Dillon didn't eat much candy, but he did. Too much, he supposed. As he exited the elevator to go to her room, he saw Kari and the baby coming toward him. Smiling, she handed him little Aster. Landon showed her to his grandda.

"I think they're going to release her today. The doctor is very impressed with how well she is doing." Landon asked her if she was kidding. "No. They got her up out of the bed and she was moving around. Slowly, but moving. And she is in much better spirits than she had been. You told her about her dad, right?"

"Yes. Last night when I came back to see her. She said it was all right." They had hit the lotto when it came to parents. All of them had, he supposed. "I'm ready to take her home. Earl is going to be excited too. He's come on as our butler."

"Wonderful. Do you think he'll make me some of his cookies? I have never had a better chocolate chip than his. And so thick with them too. I swear I could eat a dozen of them." Landon said that he'd make sure she had some when he baked next time. "Good. Thank you."

Entering her room, Landon was happy to see that Dillon was sitting in her chair and eating her lunch. Soon, he told himself, they'd be in their own home and they could move on with their lives.

He told her what he'd done today, even telling her about what he'd taken from his parents' house. In regards to the house, she thought that he should offer Drew the same deal that he'd been given when Alexandra had sold him hers. He thought that was an excellent idea, but might have a hard time convincing Drew.

"I don't think you will. I think, like the rest of you guys, you want to have your own home. And I have heard from

Kari that he spends more time alone than any one of you guys." He said that he had no idea why, but Drew seemed to enjoy his solitude. "I think he's lonely. I mean, I know he chooses to live like he does, but I think it's more of a habit now rather than him wanting to be alone. If he gets this house and a wife, he might change. I guess you guys have a little."

"For the best. I know that Steele is...I was going to say softer, but that's not it. He's still hard, but not like he was before. Steele was cold, heartless, and I wondered at times why he didn't kill himself when all this happened to him." Dillon told him what she'd heard. "I can see Aster holding him to that. Making him promise to be strong. It explains a great deal about why he was like he was. There was this promise hanging over him."

"He loves his sister very much. Not many people get the chance to be with them, even after they're gone." Landon nodded and looked at his grandda. He had no idea what he might have done had he not been there for him. "Landon, I want to have children. Like soon. I want to hold them in my arms, love on them the way we never were. Raise them to be happy and honest human beings, and teach them that not all people are like their grandparents. Excluding your grandda, of course."

"I'd love that. Very much." He moved to the bed and lay down with her. "We should make sure we start right away. I mean, when we get home, we can start on that."

"We already did." He lay there nodding before his grandda started laughing. Landon sat up and started to ask him what was wrong when he realized what Dillon had said.

"What?" She repeated it. "We're pregnant? I mean you're pregnant? Right now? You're going to have a baby right now?"

"Well, not at this moment, no, but in about seven months. I think I might have conceived in the front seat of your truck." Landon looked at her belly and then at her face, battered still and bruised. "I'll be fine. I talked to the doctor today and he said that everything is just fine with the baby, and we'll have a nice pregnancy."

Landon picked her up off the bed and swung her around. "Grandda, did you hear that? We're going to be parents. You're going to be a great grandda. Oh my God, I have to tell Steele. And Kari. I have to...oh hell, baby, I love you."

Landon held Dillon until she fell asleep. Grandda had left them at some point, telling him that he had some people to tell too. Landon closed his eyes and let sleep take him, realizing for the first time he'd not been plagued by nightmares in a very long time.

CHAPTER 12

Danny was there, she knew it, but Dillon had no idea where he wanted her to look. There was nothing. Not a thing that she could do to help him find his head. She looked at Addie when she giggled.

"You should see yourself right now. You have no idea whether you want to hit him or cry. I know just how you feel. How the hell Kari did it, being pregnant for nine months and not killing someone because of hormones, is beyond me." Addie was going to have a baby too. It was as if they'd all drank from the same well, as Connie had said to Landon. "I'm helping. It's just that the man is really upset, but I think that it's more than he has no head. I don't know what it is, but he's been acting weird since we got here."

"I have no idea if he's not been weird all along, but I do have a question for you. How is he talking to you?" Addie asked her what she meant. "I mean, he has no head. Which stands to reason that he also has no mouth. How the hell is he telling you how upset he is?"

"His body has no head. He does as a ghost." Dillon nodded, still not sure what the hell she was doing here, but she knew that this was where the man was buried. "He swears to me that his head isn't around here. But I think it's more than that. It's...I think he's lying to you about this. Why would he not want you to find it if you're sure it's here?"

"I don't know, but I think you're right. There is no reason for me to believe that he ever had a head other than his say so." Addie laughed again and Dillon told her she didn't want to know what he said now. "I'm looking for it, but even when I touch something that was yours and only yours, all I'm getting is dead air."

She actually thought about telling him perhaps that was the problem, that he was full of hot air, but didn't. He was upset enough. But they had been out here on this land that his family said was his for three hours, and she was hot and hungry. Just as she was ready to call it a day, she felt something.

Moving slowly in a small circle, she knew that something was close, that he was here and lying to them. It might be nothing but the change from his pants that had fallen out, but whatever it was, it was calling to her. Moving in a wider circle, just about a foot wider than before, she knew that she was getting closer.

"He said to tell you you're in the wrong place." She said that she wasn't. "He's pretty insistent. He thinks you're about ten feet to the left too far away."

She wasn't, she knew it. As she widened her circle, Dillon stopped moving. It was here. Well, maybe not his head, but there was something here that belonged to him. As she asked Drew to help her out with the digging, he told her to step back and let him do it. They'd all been treating her like a fragile doll since she'd come home from the hospital.

"Let him." She looked at Addie before letting her temper go on the man. "They know what you looked like when they brought you into the hospital a few weeks ago. As long as it's still fresh in their mind, I think you should let them work this out on their own. Drew especially."

"Why Drew?" She nodded toward him. He was digging the hole where she'd told him like a man who was possessed. She noticed that he did everything that way. He was so single minded sometimes that she wondered how he could walk and chew gum at the same time. "Do you think someone hurt him?"

"Yes. Badly too. And not just mentally, though that's bad enough. But he's scarred too." As soon as he hit something hard, Addie laughed again. "Your ghost is pretty pissed off. I don't think he meant for you to find his head at all."

"Why not?" Addie just shrugged. Dillon moved to where a medium-sized trunk was being pulled from the hole and looked down at the lock on it. She asked Addie if she knew what was in it.

"It's his head. And I was right. He never wanted you to find it. I think he's been enjoying being with you, aggravating you to get it finished. Even though he knew where it was all the time, it was a game for him. To spend time with you." Dillon pointed out that she wasn't able to see him. "No, but he just liked being with you. He wants to help you."

"Help me what?" Addie told her. "I'm not a necromancer. I can't see the dead. How does he figure this will work?"

"I don't know. But he wants you to open the trunk." Dillon said she wasn't going to do it. "Danny said that you won't see his head. It's been wrapped up in a large blanket and taped. He said that he knew it all along, but liked you too much to let you know."

Dillon looked at Drew. "What do you think? Open it or just take it to his family to bury? I don't know what to do, if you want to know the truth."

"What if there is something in there that they shouldn't see?" She asked him what. "I don't know. His entire porn collection. He says that's not it, but he's lied to you all along. So I think I'd open it, see what's there, and if it's not his head, you don't have to upset his family more with it."

So they took the lock off. It had taken an ax to cut through it, but once they had it open, they had to wait about an hour for the odor to dissipate and they could go near it. There was little doubt that something dead was in the box. Holding her shirt up over her nose, she looked down into the chest.

His head was wrapped in a thick blanket that was in a plastic bag. And she could see some of the bodily fluids that had leaked out of it and were on the bottom. Next to it was a smaller box, and it had her name on it. She looked at Addie.

"Why is my name here? Why is it...who wanted me to find this?" Addie turned to look beside her, and Dillon looked around. If he'd brought her out here for her father to find, he was well and too late for that. When Addie laughed again, she thought perhaps she might be inclined to murder her and stuff her in a box, but Drew laughed as well.

"He knew that you'd find him, so he took the body of the man that had hidden him here and asked him to leave this for you. It's not bad, he promises." She asked Drew if he'd said what was in it. "No. He said that it's for you to open. Something...he's not saying. I swear."

Drew reached into the box and pulled out the smaller one. She just knew it was going to be his dick or something, and tried to think how to not open the stupid thing. But knowing that she had to, she finally slipped the little lever over and opened it.

"Oh my." She looked at Addie, then at Drew. "It's beautiful. It's...it's just simply beautiful."

The cameo broach was nestled in a bed of the prettiest yellow silk she'd ever seen. Bright and cheery, she wanted to rub it against her cheek to see if it was as soft as it looked. But the cameo, old and nearly as big as her palm, was laying there as if it had been waiting all this time for her to find. Taking it out of the box, she realized that it wasn't a brooch but a necklace. And the chain was as delicate as she'd ever seen.

"I'd say that belonged to someone a very long time ago." Dillon nodded and Drew said he'd help her put it on. But she was almost afraid to, fearful of breaking it. But once it was on her throat, she turned and looked at Drew. "Very beautiful. For a very beautiful woman."

Dillon asked Danny where it had come from. Addie answered her, but she was just as touched by what he said as Dillon was.

"It was his great-grandmother's. The only thing he had left of her. He said that should his children know about it, they'd sell it off to the highest bidder and spend the money on something like a television or a game. He said that his mother gave it to him, telling him to give it to someone very special, and once he'd met you, there could have been no one else." Dillon asked about his wife. "She isn't any better than his children, he said."

When the police arrived some ten minutes later, neither she nor the other two mentioned the necklace. It felt warm on her skin, and she couldn't wait to show it to Landon.

"He should have been here with you. It's really too bad that the lawyer could only get him in to see his parents today." Dillon nodded at Addie. "He didn't want you to go?"

"No. That's why I went ahead and did this today. To keep me from worrying about him. He really didn't want to go to see them, and I don't blame him at all. But he has his grandda, and as much as the man loves his grandson, he dislikes his son and his wife that much more." Dillon put her hand on the necklace. "Do you suppose that Danny will move on now, or will he really help me out?"

"He's there with you now. Not really sitting with you, but close. He asked me to tell you he was sorry for all this. But he really did mean well." She nodded, touched that he'd go to such lengths to befriend her. "Did you know that most of the dead know who you are? They talk about how you can help me find things. Most of them are taking bets that you're going to be working with Steele and the rest of them soon."

"I don't know what I can do. If they have an object that needs to be found, I can do that all right, but I can't talk to the dead like they can."

"I don't think it'll matter to them. Some of them, like Danny here, are missing parts of what they left behind. I don't mean heads or things like that, but a pen that they might have wanted someone to have. A letter they want found and can't remember where it is. There are all sorts of things you can do to help us." Dillon had no idea, but she said she'd like to try. "Did you know that Vinnie wants you to come and help her find things as well? She has a drawer full of one ofs. I mean, like single earrings and watches without the fobs. Just little things, but she has a feeling that they're out there, just not where. I think it would be good for you in that you're not looking for the dead, as they are all the time."

She thought it would too. Looking for lost children to find them not only dead, but by the hand of the people that were supposed to care for them, had taken its toll on her before. She'd not had a breakdown, but it had been close. Taking some time away from that might be what she needed. As they made their way back to her house, Dillon thought of nothing else.

~~~

Landon could not believe his mother. He'd thought his father was insane, but his mother was making demands of him that he...just wow, was all he could think about. She asked him if he was listening to her.

"Yes. I just...I guess I'm just slightly confused why you think I'd do any of this for you. I mean, I can understand the nicer towels, but I'm not buying you monogrammed ones. Nor am I going to go out and have custom sheets made for you. In fact, I'm not going to do any of this for you. At all. What I don't understand, and perhaps you can tell me, is why the hell you think I should." He looked down at the list he'd been given when he came in. It actually said *My Demands* on it, like he was going to rush right out and fulfill it. "You do know that you're in prison and will be for the rest of your natural life? And for the better part of my life, you kept me in one too. Just by treating me the way you and Father have."

"Oh, grow up, Landon. I'm not going to stay here forever. Not if I can help it, I'm not. And that's another thing. I want you to get me better living arrangements. I hate this place. There are no rugs on the floor, nor do I have any privacy when I have to use the bathroom. This place is a dump." His father had asked for the same thing. No—*demanded*, as his mother did, that he do something about getting him out of here. Saying that not only did he not belong there, but that someone was going to pay for him being treated like this. "Who do you know that can make this happen? I'm not happy to be here."

"That's really too bad. And if you want to know the truth, Mother, if I could, I'd make it worse for you." She looked at him as if she couldn't believe he'd say such a thing to her. "As for this list? Since you didn't answer me, I'm assuming you have no real reason why I should bend over backwards to do any of this. So I'm not going to."

"Then why are you here? Why did you bother wasting my time, as you have all your life, coming here and bothering me? I swear to you, you are as useless to me now as you were as a child. Sending you away was the best idea that your father had. Especially since there was no way for us to get rid of you any other way." She slammed her hands on the table, as best she could being chained to it, and told him to get to the list. "Damn it, will you please grow some balls and get this shit taken care of for me? It's the very least you could do after all we've suffered for you. And don't think you're going to get too cozy in my house either. I don't care what that will said, you're not entitled to a damned thing."

"Really? Then no. No. You can rot in here for all I give a shit. I'm not going to lift a finger to help you, to bring you anything, nor am I going to try and find a way for you to get to somewhere nicer. You're here, deal with it." She called him a few names, no worse than he'd heard before, as he just sat there.

"If you can't be grateful that we brought you into this world, then I'd rather you just didn't visit me as much." He told her he wasn't coming back. "Then how do you expect me to know when you've made progress on my list? You don't really think you're not going to do those things, Landon. We're Logans, and we do not do well in prison like this. You think these ignorant people are going to come and tell me? They won't even let me have my own phone in here. I have to use the one in the hall like I'm some sort of criminal and might steal it."

"You are a criminal, Mother. You killed your own father, as Father did his. You also lied to me about him. As well as you continued to blame me for the fire at the school when you knew from the beginning that I had nothing to do with it." She shrugged. "Why? Why did you make me go on believing that I had caused that fire when it was a meth lab blowing up? What reason could you have had for that?"

"It kept you away, didn't it? Kept you in line and away from us. Shamed you into believing you were never good enough for us. Which, I might add, I never thought you were anyway. From the moment you were given to me at the hospital, after all that labor and pain, I knew you were going to be a disappointment, and as you can see, I was right." She pointed to the list. "Get that done, Landon, or so help me, I will make you regret it."

Instead of sparring with her any more, he stood up. He'd had enough. Between his father telling him how good it had been to kill his own father after that will he'd made them sign, to the demands of wanting Landon to give him enough money that he could pay the guards while he made a few bucks. His father even wanted to smuggle him in some drugs, saying this was the perfect place to set up a nice little business. His mother said his name as he was nearly to the door.

"When will you be back, Landon? I'm not going to just sit here and wait for some news, as little as I get to come to me through the channels. I demand that I start seeing some improvements to my living conditions right away. Make it happen before you return, or don't bother returning." He told her he wasn't coming back. "Why are you doing this to me? I deserve better than this. I deserve more than you ever gave me, that's for sure."

"You deserve exactly what you got. And as I told Father, if I could, I'd make sure you not only didn't have a cot to sleep on, but nothing in the way of luxuries either."

She was still screaming at him when he left the room. He had no idea what the guard was saying to her, but his voice was getting just as loud as hers was as the door slammed shut behind him. Going to the desk to turn in his badge, Landon felt lighter. His entire body felt like a giant weight had been lifted from his shoulders as well. Going out into the sunshine, he looked at Steele when he stood. The only person that he wanted with him when this ordeal started had come with him, even though he'd told him he didn't want him to.

"Dillon called." He nodded as he handed him his cell phone. He'd not been allowed to take it in, and saw no reason to miss a call just because his parents had decided to talk to him. "Did it go as badly as you thought it would?"

"Worse." He told him what they both had wanted. "Sounds like something my mother would have said. When I went to see her, after I left, it was like I'd been set free."

"That's what I feel now. And I told both of them I wasn't coming back either." Steele nodded as they made their way to his truck. "Steele, do you think they made us what we are? I don't mean necromancers, but I mean, personally? I know that was asked before, but I'd really like an answer if you have one."

"You mean broken until we found someone to love us? If that's what you mean, then I hope so. It's wonderful to think that something good came from having a family like them." Landon nodded and thought of Drew and Hugh, and wondered briefly what was in store for either of them. "You okay?"

"I actually think that I am now. It's like...well, we were none of us very easy to love, yet we found it. We're not really very social, and we certainly have our own kind of baggage that has nothing to do with the ghosts we have with us." Steele agreed with him. "I'm in love with my wife and we're going to have a baby. I think that's about the best one could hope for under any circumstances, don't you?"

"Yes."

Steele had driven, so Landon got into the passenger side and called Dillon. She told him that she'd finally found Mr. Crenshaw's head, and what he'd said about working for them. He relayed the information to Steele.

"Tell her that's a wonderful idea. And I think it's good that she's going to work with all of us as well." He told her what Steele said, and she laughed as she spoke again.

"I love you. I don't tell you that often enough, I don't think." Landon told her that he was in love with her as well. "Since you seem to not be talking about your parents and the visit, I can assume that it went about as well as you'd thought it would. I wish I could have been there with you."

"Had you come, I'm sure that I'd be bailing you out of jail about now. My mother was especially caustic about her demands." He told her a few of the things that they'd wanted. "Mother even told me that I owed her for not killing me as a baby."

He heard Steele hiss out his anger but continued talking to Dillon. When she laughed, he felt his heart soar in happiness and wondered how he'd lived this long without it. Landon asked her what she was going to do now.

"I'm not sure. Vinnie wants me to help her out at the shop. And I think I might like that. And Addie said that I could find things for your clients as well. She said that she thinks that finding children all the time is not good." He agreed and told her so. "I'm going to help out the police like I have been, but I think I'm going to be more selective about what I do. It's really stressful knowing what parents did to their children."

"I'm glad." Landon asked her about the arrangements with her father. His body had been in the coroner's office for three weeks now, and they'd finally released it a few days ago. "His attorney, Garrett, has been making noises about this will that says he gets everything, but as far as the courts are concerned, there isn't one. I'm not sure what he thought was going to happen with that because he's in jail and going off to prison for a long time after his trial for kidnapping, as well as a bunch of other stuff. But the judge ruled that the one he wrote on his deathbed is going to stand. I don't want any of his crap, if you want to know the truth."

"Then we'll sell it off. I don't care. It's not like we need it." Lee had told him his net worth today after all was said and done, and he was as wealthy as Steele was. "If you want, we can donate the money to some cause that your father would have hated. Whatever you want to do, I'll support you fully."

"Good. I like your idea about the hotel and want to do that with it. He would have hated having strangers in his house." Landon told her that he'd help her do it. "I'm going to give the city enough funds to build and maintain a house for kids on the edge. Not just people who see ghosts, though we won't call it that, but anyone that needs for someone to believe in them. It'll be a halfway house, sort of, until they can come to grips with what they are."

"I love that idea. Think of how many lives it might save just to have somewhere for people to go and talk." She said that she had no idea how to get it started, but she was going to look into it. "Good. I'm sure that we can get enough support around to keep it running. There has to be someone that we can trust to do so."

"Drew said he would help me." Landon looked at Steele when Dillon told him that. Drew had been pulling from them for a long time now, and he wondered aloud to Steele if this was the final straw.

"I hope not, but there couldn't be a better person to run that place." Landon agreed. "It's not like he's going to be that far away if we need him for something. A simple car ride and he's right here. I like the idea."

"Good. I knew that the two of you would." Dillon said she had to go and would see him soon. He put his cell away and looked at Steele when he laughed.

"Could be that this is just what Drew needs to bring him around." Landon asked him if he knew what had happened to Drew. "I do. But...it's not a story that I think I should tell. He's been...hurt doesn't even begin to cover what happened to him. Makes what happened to us seem like child's play. But this might help him."

Landon hoped so. His friend was hurting a great deal.

CHAPTER 13

Drew woke. He knew better than to even move his toe if he knew what was good for him. His hand, down by his side, didn't so much as twitch in fear as he lay there, darkness covering him like a thick hot fudge sauce that seemed to not just be over him, but in every pore of his body as well. Digging his finger deep into the mattress, he knew that he wasn't locked away but in a bed. Not that it made things any better for him.

The house made the usual sounds that one did when it was old and needed repair. Nothing that he wasn't familiar with, but the same as he'd heard in every night of his life. That included the hospital that he'd spent nearly three months in when he'd been ten. It didn't lessen his fear, but seemed to compound it as things around him began to take shape in his fertile mind.

"It's time you got your lazy ass up, don't you think?" The voice nearly made him scream. He did whimper at the sound, the first noise he'd made since he'd opened his eyes. "I'm waiting for you."

"Please. Just go away. Can't you just leave me alone?"
The voice—a woman's he knew as well as his own, the sound
of it dark and raspy like a man's—laughed at him. "Please?"

"You can't wish that for me, boy. This place is mine until
I say different. Now get your lazy ass out of that bed. You
have to get me some shit. You're not smart enough to care
for yourself, now are you?" The movement of the voice had
him turning in that direction, his body no less relaxed
knowing that the woman in his room was his own dead
mother. "I have always cared for you, Andrew, and I always
will. Till death do we part. And if you don't do what I tell
you, that might be sooner than you think. Boy? Are you
testing me?"

"Like you took care of me on my tenth birthday." He
knew he'd made a mistake the moment the words left his
mouth. Her energy, hot and heavy, washed over him. The
lights in the room, even off, popped in their housing and
shattered glass in their wake. She was strong, even in her
death. "I'm leaving here. I want you to know that, and when
I do, I'm having this house taken care of."

"No you won't. You got nowhere to go and no one to
care for you." He'd bought a house. From Landon, and he'd
be living there today if things went the way he wanted them
to. Not in this place where the walls still bore the evidence of
his mother's fury that fateful night. "Now, Andrew. I don't
want to hear any more talk about you thinking you're going
to leave me. I want you to get the house back to the way it
was. I told you before, I don't care for you messing with my
shit. Or do you have to go to work? Then I want you to go
out and get me some shit. I need a score bad."

"I'm...this is my last night here. The last time you will be
able to speak to me. To terrorize me." He was flirting with
danger now, he knew that. His body, sitting up, now ached

for what she'd done to him all those years ago. "I'm not coming back here either. I've decided to destroy this house."

"You can't unless I say you can, you hear me?" Her anger was hotter now. The heat of it burned into his flesh where he had feeling, and he thought of that night again. "Now, you're to stop this talk and do what I tell you to do. Backtalk will get you hurt. I'd think you'd know that by now. I should like for you to tell me what you are going to do in the back gardens. I want you to plant me some weed. I can sell it or trade it for some better shit." Her voice was hard, unforgiving, as it always was when she didn't get her way.

"There are no back gardens. I sold that off long ago to take care of your bills and other things that came up. Remember?" He got up out of the bed, moving slowly until he could get his flesh to even out, become more elastic. "I told you this before. It's been sold off for the new development that is coming in."

"I'd like you to start on the weed today. Get it surrounded by some tall plants back there. You can buy them online, I'm told. That way if them assholes come along and think to have a looksee in the back, all they'll see is my simpleton son planted some posies." Drew ignored her in favor of taking a shower. But her voice followed him in the tiny room even when she didn't enter. "Once you get the seeds in the ground, then I can put the word out that I'm in business. I'll have them lined up out the door then. I don't remember the name of the guy you usually work with for me. Do you remember? Never mind. You can just order the plants and I'll work on the rest."

"There is nothing around this house but dead grass. And the trees are gone as well." Turning on the water, knowing that this was his last shower here as well, he stripped down after shutting the door and turned on the light.

This room, like all the rooms in the house, had no mirror. There was a small one in the hall just by the door, but it had been covered up for so long that he rarely thought of it any more. If he needed to look at himself, he usually waited until he was at someone else's house or at a public restroom, but never here. And never naked.

Scrubbing his body, Drew thought of what he had to do today. The house, like most of the houses on this block, was being torn down in the name of development. He'd been the only hold out until two weeks ago, and now he was as ready to be gone as the others had been. The only difference was, Drew was leaving everything but a few things he'd given away. He wanted nothing from the house that he'd grown up in. There was nothing here but horrible memories, and scars so deep that he'd never been able to look at himself fully in twenty years.

As he exited the bathroom, the hot water already gone, he pulled out his only pair of pants, a new pair that he'd purchased just for this occasion, and pulled them on. His mother would be gone now, down in the kitchen wondering what to do about making him something to eat. The food was gone too, donated to the local pantry, along with the freezer and its contents that had been nearly empty as well. Not that she could cook, but she did make a fuss over him as he did it for himself.

She was standing in the kitchen looking out over the yard just as he'd thought she would be. He didn't doubt that she was counting the money that was never going to come in. His mother had never done a damned thing when she didn't have to, including caring for him as she should have. Whether there was money for it or not, and if he was still hungry after she got her fill, she told him to make due. Drew had made due a lot by stealing what he'd needed.

Not speaking to her, not wanting to get into another discussion that was pointless and had been said many times before, he picked up his jacket and moved to the door. Without a backward glance, he was out the door and to his car in minutes. The big earth movers were already tearing down the house next to his, and he had to smile.

His new house wasn't far from Steele's, just about two miles down the road. And it was pretty close to Landon and Dillon. Three days ago he'd gone to the mall and purchased himself all new clothing, including a new coat and shoes, something that he'd not bought in a long time. Then he'd gotten himself pillows and sheets for the new bed. His house was really too big for him, but it was his now. And all because Landon had been a good friend to him.

"I'd like to sell you my parents' house. For a buck." Drew told him no, he didn't want it. "You need it as much as I need to sell it to you. It comes furnished as well. And there is a cook. Her name is Anna Reeves. She's nice. A little on the odd side, but nice."

"I don't want a house. I have one." Landon asked him how much longer he thought that was going to work out for him. "I don't know, but I don't want your house."

"If you buy it from me, then I'll tell Dillon to stop looking into what makes you like you are." Drew started to deny anything she might find. "You know she will. I did. And I wasn't even looking all that hard. She'll find it. Then what do you think she'll do?"

"I don't want her sympathy. And I certainly don't need it." Landon said nothing. "Why didn't you just ask me?"

"Would you have told me?" Drew said nothing. "Didn't think so. But I knew some dates, and just plugged them in to see what happened. I'm assuming that the others have no idea either."

"I'd like to keep it that way too. No one...what the fuck am I supposed to do now? I don't want the fucking house, but I don't want her getting into my life either." Landon had just stared at him. "You're not helping me."

"Oh, but I am. I am helping you as much as you'll be helping me. Buy the house and be happy. Well, as happy as you can be." Drew wanted to hit him but didn't. He had been having a bad day, and the pain was just barely controlled then. "Lee will be contacting you in the morning. I've already had the paperwork changed over to your name. Congratulations. Here is the key."

After Landon had left him sitting in the restaurant, he sat there for an hour nursing a beer that he'd not taken a single drink of. When he realized that he was well and truly fucked in this, he snatched up the keys and went to his car. The moment he saw the house, he knew that it was going to be perfect for him.

There were no neighbors to speak of. The house sat on about seventy acres of wooded land. The privacy fence around it was tall enough to keep out the most persistent of people, and he knew that it had a guard on it, a magic safety net that Steele would have put on it the moment that Landon told him he'd sold him the house. He moved into the front door and was surprised to see that the house really was furnished.

The entire bottom floor looked like a showcase for a magazine spread. There were flowers in vases that looked fresh, art in frames that looked as old as the house was. When someone cleared their throat, he'd turned, expecting to see his mother, when a smallish woman smiled at him.

"I'm Anna Reeves, sir. You must be the new owner." There was no point in denying it, so he nodded. "Mr. Landon said you'd be by today. That I was to have you a list of things that the kitchen needed. I must say that it's well stocked, and there is little other than food that we'll be needing."

"Steele, Steele Bennett, he uses this service that brings out groceries, unless you want to go and get them." She said that she'd like that. "I'll make sure that you have credit set up, then. Just get everything that you need and we'll go from there."

"Good sir. I've a daughter that would like to come and work with me, if you don't mind. I can pay her. She's got herself a good head on her shoulders, and is in need of some extra cash for her books and such. She's in her last year of college to be a nurse." Drew told her that he'd pay her a good wage too. "Thank you, sir."

"Call me Drew. I'm not sure how this works, you working for me, but I don't want it to be too formal. I'm just a simple man who likes his privacy." She said she understood. "I won't be having parties or people over. And I want to be left alone as much as possible."

"Very good, sir...Drew. I can work with that." After they had worked out a way for her to contact him before he was moved in, she made her way to the kitchen and he finished his tour of the house. By the time he was done, he knew that despite the fact that he was forced into the deal, he was glad that it was his. The house called to him.

And today he was finally moving in.

As he made his way up the long drive, he thought about what his mother was going to do now. Not that he really cared. He just didn't want her coming to him. Not now, not ever again. The fact that she'd been unable to leave the house that she'd killed herself in wasn't his doing but her own, and he hoped that she never figured out that she could move. But now that her resting place was going to be destroyed, he knew that she'd not be long for this world. At least he hoped so.

Andrew Mullins was finally and hopefully forever free from the woman that had made him what he was today. A necromancer that, because of her trying to kill him and succeeding twice while he'd been set on fire, was going to try and get on with his life. Whatever that might be.

~~~

Stupid people were around today. Ryder Mackenzie, Mac to her friends, watched the couple as they struggled to get their kayak in the water without getting their very expensive shoes wet. Not going to happen, she thought. They were in the fucking water and they were going to get wet. As she made her way around them and to the couple she was going to work with for the next couple of hours, she wondered again what the fuck she was going to do this winter. Other than a planned visit to see her best bud since college, she was at a loss. Maybe she'd take a cruise, she thought with a grin. Never going to happen was her next thought.

As she told the couple how to maneuver the small boat and how to guide themselves through the water, her mind drifted. Mac had been doing this for so long, kayaking down this particular river, she could have drawn a map for them about every single rock they needed to avoid, as well as all the places that would tip them if they didn't use their oars just right. And this was not the only river she could do that to.

"Will you be going with us?" She wanted to tell them that if they were stupid enough to think that she was going to just let them go in the water alone, then they had no business doing this, but only nodded. "Good. I have a feeling that we're going to need a great deal of help before the day is out."

"You'll be fine." And not that she was conceited or anything, but she knew that they would be because she was there. "I've done this over a million times. Once we get to the first bend, you'll wonder why you never did it before."

They all watched the couple with the expensive shoes go by them. Roger was their guide, and he looked at her like he wanted her to save him. Instead, she waved at him and gave him the thumbs up, something that they did even when they knew it was going to be a disaster. And that trip had that written all over it.

As she got into her own kayak and moved it into the slow moving water, she kept an eye on the couple she was with. They were trying, she had to give them that. And not doing a bad job of it either. They were both soaked by the time they were twenty feet from where they'd started, and laughing like they had not a care in the world. She reached up and turned on her camera at her helmet and told them to do the same. She thought this couple would love a copy of their day. By the end, she was enjoying herself as much as they seemed to be.

"It was amazing, and you were right, we did wonder why we didn't try it before now." Nodding at them, she smiled, but her mind was elsewhere. Roger wasn't back yet. That did not bode well for any of them. As soon as she was able to detach herself from the couple, she went to the security office to see if they had any idea where he was.

"They're on the last leg, but don't seem to be getting anywhere fast." She asked Sandy what she meant. "They won't budge any further. They're telling Roger that no one told them it was going to be this hard or that they'd get wet."

"Yeah, right. You're in the middle of the fucking river. What did they expect to happen?" Sandy laughed. "Can you get in touch with him for me?"

As soon as Roger got on the two-way with her, she knew that he was about at his wits end. His anger was enough to make her smile just a little. She asked him how it was going.

"These motherfuckers are claiming that I took them to the only part in the river where they'd get wet, and then I made them do all the work. How the fuck was I supposed to make it so that they did all the work, I ask you? It's a one person boat, for fuck sake." Mac asked him what he was going to do. "Nothing. Leave their asses here. Hope they can flag down someone that can bring them back, and charge them double for pissing me off."

"I'm on my way." He didn't say anything, and she figured he wasn't going to argue with her about what she said next either. "Leave them. I'll be there in about twenty minutes or so depending on conditions. All right?"

"Yeah, but you should know that they're calling themselves in a lawyer. I have no idea what they expected, but they got him on the line right now." She told him she wasn't worried. "But I am. I can't be out of work right now, Mac. I just bought me a house, and I got Adie in college this year. I just can't afford this."

"You know I have your back, Roger. Don't worry. Just tell them that you're coming in here, and if they want to come, then that's fine. Otherwise, just go. I'll take care of it all." He thanked her and told her he'd let her know when he was on the water and if they came with him. "And Roger, don't tell them to take the cameras off. We want as much as we can get with them and their idiotic ideas."

Twenty minutes later, he called her back to tell her that he'd left them. "They're powerful mad, just so you know.

Telling me that I'm on their list of people to sue. Even the owner is going to feel their wrath. Also, they said they were going to give us a review that will knock our socks off. I don't think they mean that in a good way either."

After assuring him that she was going to handle it, she got in her own kayak and moved into the water. When there was no one with her Mac could make amazing time, and was pulling into the area where the Smithys were about fifteen minutes later. Mac knew this area better than most people knew their own yards. This was, she thought, her own yard.

"Mr. and Mrs. Smithy." The man launched himself at her and she sidestepped him just as he lunged at her. Mac was in much better shape than him and only had to sidestep him a little, then give him a little push for him to end up on his ass. She grinned at him when he started cursing at her. "Not a nice way to treat someone that has come to get you back. Now. This is how we're going to do this. You're going to—"

"You're going to listen to me, is what you're going to do. I want you to have a helicopter come in and get us. Then I want you to have that owner of yours write us a check. A nice fat one with lots of zeros after the number. Then we'll think about not suing your ass for leaving us out here without means to protect ourselves."

"From what?" He looked confused. "What is it you think you need to be protected from? The biggest prey we have around here is mosquitoes, and those aren't so bad this time of year. Spring is the worst, but we're into fall and they're not around so much. The fish? Well, since you haven't been in the water, I think we can rule that out. What is it you need protecting from?"

"That man never told us we'd get wet." Mac looked at Mrs. Smithy and then at the water. When she looked back at the woman, she actually stomped her foot. "I paid two hundred dollars for these shoes, and almost that much for my outfit. Just look at me. I'm a mess."

"Yeah, happens when you do a little work. And you did see all the signage in the office that said 'you will get wet,' didn't you? Then there was the waiver. Also, inside the kayak, there's at least three signs there that say that you'll be wet. And also, there is the added fact that you're in water using an oar. Pretty sure that it would be a given to most that you're going to get wet." The man growled at her. "In the event you're confused on how this is going to work, I'll tell you. You're either going to get in those boats and move yourself down the river, or I'm going to leave you here. Alone. No one will come back for you, and I will not call in any chopper to come and get you. Not that anyone would. This is pretty remote even for them. It's the river, or you stand here until you get it in your head to make it back. Oh, and since these kayaks belong to Extreme, they're leaving with me. With or without you."

"You'd just leave us here. With no way of getting back." She told the man that she would and have no problem with it. "I'm going to own that company you work for. See if I don't."

"In order to do that, you're going to have to get back to the land of the living. And that's not going to happen any time soon if you don't get your butts in the boats and move with me. Because as of right now, you have five minutes to decide. And once I'm gone, so is your means of moving to where your car is."

Mac set her watch and then went to her own boat. She was just pulling away when the couple, pissed as fuck, moved to climb into theirs. She had no idea if it was anger or just plain nastiness, but they made pretty good time getting back to the area where the buses would pick them up.

"They're on their way. Did Harmon show up yet?" Their attorney for the company was also one of the teachers. He didn't work for them much on the river, just a way for him to get some exercise, he told her, to burn off the office ass, but he did a lot of work for them when they needed legal help, and she let him ride for free.

"Yes, he's here. As is their friend. He's not an attorney, but he is acting like he is. I sent Roger home. He was pretty upset." She told her thanks. "Also, you should know that we're full up in the morning, so if you can make it in before that, I'll bring in some donuts."

Telling her to take money out of the petty cash, Mac told her that she was going on home. It was only another four miles downriver, and she was just too tired to deal with going back to the office. As she got into her kayak and started out, she thought of all the things she wanted to do next week when she was off. An entire week off to drive out to see her friend Addie Stark. They were going to have a good time, she hoped. Ten minutes later, she was hearing what she thought was loud laughter.

Only it wasn't fun and games as she'd thought. The screams had her pausing in her rowing. Looking to her left, she could see the people in the large raft. They were pointing downstream, screaming at someone in the water, and that was when Mac saw it. The child.

It was bobbing up and down in the water like a bobber on a line. And the two people that were moving quickly away from the child were in as much if not more trouble than they knew. The falls, about fifty feet from them, were coming up fast. Mac pulled her headset down and called for help.

"Three in water, one child, two adults. No life jackets on adults that I can see, child in arm bubbles and some sort of vest. Near the bend at Winding Row. Mackenzie on scene."

201

The dispatcher asked her if they needed the net. "Yes. And hurry."

She felt her back pull as she rowed faster than she had since college. Every part of her was focused on the child. The adults were going to have to fend for themselves until she could, if she could get to the child.

As she neared the falls, a place that few ever ventured over unless you really wanted a thrill, were coming up fast. The water was churning so quickly that she was having a hard time keeping the child in her sights. Just as Mac was close enough to touch her — she could see it was a little girl — her kayak wedged between two large stones. Mac grabbed up the child and noted right away that she wasn't breathing. A hard shake to free her from the tangle she was in brought a scream from her that made Mac's heart take an unexpected twist. Then the girl launched herself at Mac, and they both went over the falls.

Now Available in the Justice Series

Steele
Justice Series Book 1

Nick
Justice Series Book 2

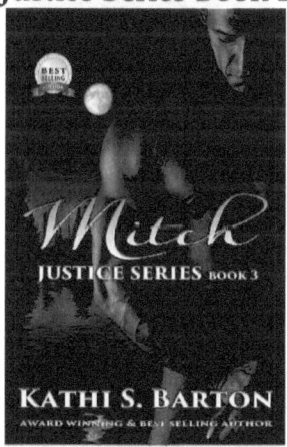

Mitch
Justice Series Book 3

Landon
Justice Series Book 4

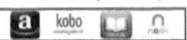

Before You Go...

HELP AN AUTHOR

write a review

THANK YOU!

Share your voice and help guide other readers to these wonderful books. Even if it's only a line or two your reviews help readers discover the author's books so they can continue creating stories that you'll love. Login to your favorite retailer and leave a review. Thank you.

Kathi Barton, author of the bestselling series Force of Nature, lives in Nashport, Ohio with her husband Paul. In addition to writing full time Kathi likes to spend time with her eight grandkids, three children and three children-in-laws. She writes to relax and have fun.

Her muse, a cross between Jimmy Stewart and Hugh Jackman brings them to life for her readers in a way that has them coming back time and again for more. Her favorite genre is paranormal romance with a great deal of spice. You can visit Kathi on line and drop her an email if you'd like. She loves hearing from her fans. aaronskiss@gmail.com.

Follow Kathi on her blog:
http://kathisbartonauthor.blogspot.com/

www.ingramcontent.com/pod-product-compliance
Lightning Source LLC
Chambersburg PA
CBHW032127170626
46808CB00006B/2138